The Lovers

Vendela Vida

Atlantic Books

London

First published in the United States of America by HarperCollins Publishers, 10 East 53rd Street, New York, NY 10022.

First published in hardback and export and airside trade paperback in Great Britain in 2011 by Atlantic Books, an imprint of Atlantic Books Ltd.

This paperback edition published in 2012 by Atlantic Books.

Peterborough City Council		
60000 0000 62638		
Askews & Holts	May-2012	
	£7.99	

1 2 3 4 5 6 7 8 9

A CIP catalogue record for this book is available from the British Library.

Paperback ISBN: 978 184887 521 0
E-book ISBN: 978 085789 505 9

Printed in Italy by Grafica Veneta SpA

Atlantic Books
An Imprint of Atlantic Books Ltd
Ormond House
26–27 Boswell Street
London
WC1N 3JZ

www.atlantic-books.co.uk

The Lovers

endela Vida is the author of the acclaimed novels
nd Now You Can Go and Let the Northern Lights
ase Your Name. She is a founding editor of the
liever magazine and the editor of The Believer Book
Writers Talking to Writers. She lives in the San
ancisco Bay Area with her husband and children.

ring and original. . . Playful and ultimately heart-
ng.' Independent on Sunday

la Vida writes with clarity and precision and a finely
sense of empathy. . . This is not just a "woman's novel";
houghtful and evocative story of what it means to love,
on loving.' Observer

f sharply-observed moments and poignant insights
he impossibilities – and possibilities – of human
tion. . . [The Lovers is] a darkly elegant book about
promises and redemption.' Guardian

nt. . . The Lovers is a moving work on the tumbling,
overwhelming emotions that follow [the] rawest of events. . .
Grief   future,
and Vi

The Lovers

When half an hour had passed and there was still no sign of a white Renault, Yvonne began to fear she'd been scammed. Her flight from Istanbul was the last of the day, and the small Dalaman airport was beginning to empty. She stood outside, under a pink-veined sky, looking for anybody who appeared to be looking for her. There was no one but taxi drivers announcing, "I take you," or miming the equivalent. She reentered the terminal, hoping she'd missed seeing Mr. Çelik's employee, who, she'd been told, would be holding a piece of paper bearing her name. But the only visible sign was a large poster on the wall: TURKEY—WHERE EAST MEETS WEST. On the poster two figures, each holding a briefcase, were walking toward each other on a bridge.

She opened her laptop to consult her last e-mail from Mr. Çelik, and immediately regretted it. A pair of young men in tracksuits were staring at her. Now a woman pushing a mop was also looking her way. Peter would have disapproved; they had traveled to nine—ten? no, eleven—countries during their twenty-six years of marriage, and he had been proud of their ability to go unnoticed. This was her first trip since his death, and already she was breaking their rules.

The laptop had been a present from her son and his fiancée, and Yvonne was sorry she'd brought it. She was sorry she owned it. She carried it with her into the ladies' restroom, where, alone, she propped it on the sink counter. She was troubled to discover she was not mistaken: Mr. Çelik had last written to say she would be picked up by one of his employees at 19:30, on the fifteenth of June, outside the Dalaman airport, and be driven to the house in Datça. His e-mail also confirmed he had received the thousand-dollar deposit she'd wired into his account. A thousand dollars! What a fool she'd been to wire so much money to secure a vacation home she'd seen only on a website. She carefully wrote down Ali Çelik's phone number on the back of her boarding pass, slipped her computer into her bag, and left the restroom. There was no pay phone in sight.

Outside in the shadeless parking lot, the heat felt thick, as though it had been compacted by the hours of the day. Not wanting to offend conservative Turks, she had flown in a loose, long-sleeved blouse and a skirt that reached beneath her calves—an outfit she had discovered was both stifling and unnecessary. No one on the plane from Istanbul wore a head scarf. The Turkish women, most of them young and wealthy, were dressed in jeans and sequined T-shirts and high-heeled sandals. The rest of the seats were occupied by

British post-grads in sundresses, Turkish men in long shorts, and Norwegian girls with tight bright shirts and nondescript boyfriends.

By the parking lot there was a narrow café and newspaper kiosk, where Yvonne asked the cashier if she could make a call. She showed him the number and he pulled a black phone out from behind the bar and dialed for her. A small act of mercy—she didn't know which numbers to leave off the long row of digits.

She was surprised when a voice answered.

"Mr. Çelik?" she said.

"Oh good, it's you," he said. His accent was negligible.

"Yes, it's me," she said.

"My man has been looking for you!" Mr. Çelik said. "Where are you?"

"Just outside the airport. At the café."

"You came out on the wrong side of the airport."

"There's another side?" she asked. "I'll walk over there."

"Please. No. You stay there. I'll call and have him come around."

"Thank you," she said. He had hung up. "Thank you," she said again, and laughed with the pleasure of relief. She had not been scammed. She was not a fool.

From the plane, Yvonne had been mesmerized by the Mediterranean, its texture like chiffon. It reminded her of a play her twins had been in when they were young. Aurelia and

Matthew had each held one end of a large swath of blue iri-
descent material, and alternated lifting and lowering it with
their tiny hands. The play was called *The Ocean*.

Now, as she stood in front of the café, Yvonne couldn't see
the water, but she could taste the salt in the air. A white car
sped up and stopped, and not one but two men, one tall, the
other taller, emerged. They looked too big for the small car.

"Hello!" she said, as though she was the one welcoming
them to her country. Both men nodded.

The driver lifted her suitcase from her side and placed it
in the backseat. He ceremoniously held the door open for
her and she slid inside. The seat was warm and sticky.

"There are two of you," she said.

"He doesn't speak English, so I am here to translate," explained the man in the passenger seat. "He work for Mr. Ali
Çelik. His name is Mehmet."

Yvonne asked the interpreter what his name was, and
when she couldn't understand his response, she asked again,
and then gave up. "How long is the drive?" she said instead.

"Three hours, maybe not so much. They remake the
roads, so maybe longer or smaller. We stop for coffee."

The car started. The men spoke to each other and laughed
and Yvonne sat in the back, next to Peter's old Samsonite.
This was her companion now.

Through the window Yvonne saw rows of squat palm
trees and turquoise minarets. The car slowed through the
town of Marmaris and passed by an endless strip of bars,

many with British flags and sunburned, sandaled tourists sitting outside, drinking beer from narrow glasses.

After Marmaris there were short stretches when water was visible, until the sun, which had been making a drawn-out exit, finally dropped. Then, only shapes, sounds—the occasional house, a barking dog. Yvonne and the two men moved quickly: the moment they reached something they left it behind. She was having difficulty understanding how the trip could take even two hours at the speed they were traveling, but suddenly, after passing no particular town or landmark, the road was unpaved, and she could feel every bump, every kilometer. "We are on Datça peninsula now," the man in the passenger seat said, turning his dented chin in her direction. "Datça the town is near the end."

Yvonne nodded into the sepia darkness.

Soon after, the car pulled into a lit and landscaped area, a restaurant with only outdoor seating. The men ordered coffee and Yvonne ordered an orange Fanta.

"How do you say *thank you?*" she asked the interpreter as they walked to a table.

"Simplest way for you is *tea and sugar*. That's what sounds like. Tea and sugar."

"Tea and sugar?" said Yvonne.

"You are welcome," he said, and laughed.

They sat at a picnic table near a short bridge that spanned a small pond. Around them, at other tables, round and square, sat couples on dates and large groups of men laughing and smoking unfiltered cigarettes. The scent was both aged and ripe.

Mehmet said something and his friend translated: "Mr. Çelik is a very powerful man."

Yvonne shrugged. "I don't know much about him."

They looked at her, as though wondering how it was possible that she was unaware of Mr. Çelik's power.

"What do you know about Turkey?" Mehmet said.

"Well, a few things," she said. "I know it's one of the most beautiful countries in the world."

Mehmet's friend smiled and translated her words. Mehmet nodded. In her travels, Yvonne had yet to meet anyone, in any country, who argued with the assessment that their country was among the most beautiful.

"What else?"

"I know that Turkey hasn't been allowed into the EU."

Mehmet understood *EU* and he and his friend began a private discussion that seemed to escalate into an argument.

"Sorry," Yvonne said.

"It's okay," the interpreter said. "We just don't agree. I think that if EU doesn't want us, then fuck EU. But Mehmet, he thinks Turkey needs to look at its past. He thinks Turkey needs to be truthful about its history."

The men continued their heated discussion in Turkish. Yvonne thought she heard *Armenia,* but she couldn't be certain. The interpreter seemed to be finding English more difficult as his frustration grew, and his attempts to include her in their conversation dwindled.

The exclusion was a relief. Yvonne pulled up the sleeves of her blouse and tucked her skirt between her knees so the warm air could touch her skin. She was enjoying the role of being the observer rather than the observed. It was only now, while sitting at this roadside restaurant on the Datça peninsula, that she fully comprehended the claustrophobia she'd experienced for the past two years. She had been under surveillance, in the way that was particular to new widows. The faculty at her high school, her students, her neighbors, the dry cleaner, the clerks at the video store—especially the clerks—had all been watching her. "How are you?" was no longer a casual question, for an ambivalent response from Yvonne could inspire gossip, which in turn triggered unsolicited phone calls and concerned visits.

Recently, whenever she was asked how she was spending a weekend, she had resorted to lying, claiming her kids or some unnamed cousins were coming to visit, so no one would be aware she was passing the time alone. Burlington, Vermont, her home for half her life—the married half—had become a dollhouse, the fourth wall removed, the vacated and cluttered rooms of her solitary existence visible for all to see. Why had she waited so long to get away?

Exhaustion hit her on the second leg of the drive, but the unpaved road prevented her from sleeping. Each time she was on the cusp, a turn or bump jostled her awake. By the time they approached Datça, the idea of rest had been shaken from her body, and her head felt hollowly alert. She recognized the sensation from her jet-lagged adventures with Peter, and, more recently, from the jagged sleep cycles that had consumed her after the funeral. Those months of nights when she would finally, exhausted of tears, fall into a sleep so deep that when she awoke, she would blink in the light, drunk with the possibility of a new day, until only a minute later the reality—Peter had been killed and was gone—tightened around her again.

Once they were in Datça, Mehmet turned and drove straight uphill for ten blocks. He stopped the car in front of a white house. Yvonne recognized its shape, though the staircase was imposing, much larger than it had looked in the photos. The stairs sullied the house's appearance like bad teeth in a wide smile. As she stepped out of the car, Yvonne could see the outline of flowers that covered the entranceway. She knew from the pictures they were purple. Bougainvillea.

Yvonne followed Mehmet up the steep set of stairs while the interpreter followed behind with her suitcase and bag. The front door opened into a tiled foyer, with a dining room and kitchen to the left, and a living room to the right. The decor was white and black with red, blue, and yellow accents. A Mondrian palette. A large red steel staircase, like a structure at a children's playground, spiraled upward and down. She had come to Turkey, land of ruins and antiquity, to stay in a modern home.

With brisk steps, the men ventured around the house. The lights turned themselves on as they entered each room. At first Yvonne thought her escorts were confirming no one was in the house, but then she understood their instincts were less protective: they were curious. Mr. Çelik was a wealthy man—their boss—and Yvonne guessed this was their first time inside his home unsupervised.

"Where does Mr. Çelik go when he rents this place?" Yvonne asked. She had stepped down into the living room, which contained a large TV, a zebra-skin rug, a blue leather couch, and, behind a locked glass case, a display of old rifles.

"He has many houses. Now he stays at his winery house," the interpreter explained. He and Mehmet were standing in front of the rifle display. Yvonne could tell they were speaking to each other about Mr. Çelik's collection with admiration and not an insignificant amount of envy.

The interpreter carried her suitcase up the red spiral stairs. "What room?" he called down.

"The master one, I guess," Yvonne said. "The big one," she added.

"You are alone," he said when he came down.

"I'm waiting for my family." Her explanation was promptly translated for Mehmet. Both men nodded. It wasn't completely a lie, but as with many untruths, it made everyone feel more comfortable.

She was handed the keys to the house and to the car—

Mr. Çelik had arranged for that as well. When she'd informed him she was considering renting a car from the agency at the airport, he'd promptly e-mailed her back, saying, "Don't waste your money. I know people."

Yvonne tipped Mehmet and his friend. "Tea and sugar," she said. They seemed pleased. She inquired how they'd be getting down the hill—as a teacher and a mother, she constantly worried about how people would get home—and the interpreter pointed to another car they had apparently parked at the house earlier. She nodded, smiled, and said good-bye. As she closed the front door behind them, she tried to inhale the fragrance of the flowers before she remembered bougainvillea had no scent.

Now she was able to explore the house on her own. She climbed the staircase to the second floor. In the center of the landing was the entrance to a large bathroom, with a shower curtain patterned with green frogs and a shelf stacked with colorful beach towels. At the back of the house were two small bedrooms, one with twin beds, the other with a single bed and an ironing board standing on its insectlike legs.

Her suitcase had been placed in the largest room, in the front of the house. The bed was covered with a thin yellow bedspread, and one wall was lined with books. Yvonne pulled back the curtains, which reminded her of a crochet dress one of her sisters had owned in grade school. She pressed her face to the glass. At the bottom of the hill lay the ocean, silent and still.

The third floor was smaller, with only a single bedroom

and a balcony. On top of the bed, a piece of exercise equip-ment, complete with black straps and silver chains, had been laid out. Yvonne couldn't identify its purpose.

She descended the staircase three floors until she was in the basement. Even with the light on, it was a dim place, full of odd tables and lamps and with a couch in the center of the room. She had ventured only a few feet from the stairs when, wary of the automatic lights that might snap off, she returned to the main floor.

By the front door sat a wooden bin, like a small boat, con-taining an assortment of women's shoes. She removed her own and tried on a pair of black sandals with short heels. Her size. They were more fashionable than the shoes she was accustomed to—Callie, her son's fiancée, would have ap-proved—and she placed her own practical shoes in the bin. She walked around, enjoying the sound the sandals made on the tile floor. *The sound of elegance*, she thought. The sound of a woman preparing for a party.

The kitchen was surgical in its sparseness, the counters bare but for an unlabeled bottle of red wine. A note was propped up against the bottle: "From my vineyard. Enjoy!" There were faces on the refrigerator door, photos of people on a yacht—all of them in their twenties and thirties, all with drinks. Which one was Mr. Ali Çelik? Which of the beautiful women was his wife? The magnets securing the photos in place read CARPE DIEM! and A MAN'S WEALTH IS MEASURED BY THE AMOUNT OF FUN HE HAS!

Yvonne opened the refrigerator. Cherries glistened inside a silver strainer. She tried one, and then another. She removed the strainer and carried it to the living room, along with a napkin and a small bowl for the pits. She had under-estimated her hunger.

From the couch, she couldn't see anything outside the window—only her own reflection. A brunette woman with pale skin and dark eyes removing pits from her mouth. At first glance, she looked younger than her fifty-three years. She tried not to be vain about this, but she was not un-proud. She had put on weight since Peter's death, and the extra pounds had filled in her wrinkles, her breasts, her hips. She stood and walked closer to the window so she could see her-self better, and then, wondering if the neighbors across the street could see her too, she took a quick step back and re-treated to the kitchen.

It had been extravagant to rent such a large house, but it had been the only appealing one available when, two months before, she had decided to make the trip. Her son, Matthew, had invited her to join him and Callie and Callie's family on the boat they were chartering from Greece to Turkey. "A pre-wedding cruise," he called it in his initial e-mail to Yvonne. Yvonne had never heard of such a thing, but she had never heard of many things Callie's family, the Campbells, were ac-customed to. Having been overly impressed by wealth when she was young, Yvonne now tried to keep a safe distance from people with money.

"We'll stop at EVERY archaeological site all the way until we get to Troy. You'll LOVE it, Mom," Matthew wrote.

Even his capital letters seemed pleading, anxious. It had taken Yvonne a moment to understand he was appealing to her presumed interest in history, the subject she had taught for thirty years. Matthew, though well-meaning, understood her on a superficial level. *Was that fair?* she wondered. Mother, teacher, historian, wife. Widow. He did not look beyond these terms, these roles. But Yvonne had not done so with her own mother either.

"I'll think about it," Yvonne wrote in response to Matthew's invitation, though she had already made up her mind not to go. But then came April, when another empty and unremarkable summer stretched before her like an endless walkway. She had no plans when school ended, nothing to do for three months. She considered teaching summer school. It seemed a good match: her strength as a teacher had been with students who needed extra help, not with the ones who excelled. The honor students were Peter's forte; if he had one flaw as a teacher, and as a parent, it was that he lacked patience with anything short of brilliance. Yvonne had discussed the possibility of summer school with George, the principal, who, during his first marriage, had dinner with Peter and Yvonne at least once a month. But George had suggested she take a break from teaching—"just for the summer," he said, his hand on her shoulder—and she knew then that if he could, George would suggest she take a more permanent hiatus.

His lack of faith in her had to do with Oliver Cromwell. On a Friday that past February, she delivered her standard lecture about Cromwell and the organization of the British Commonwealth. After the first few minutes, she'd noticed that everyone, even her least devoted student, was paying rapt attention. This was followed by snickers, and she knew something was wrong. Later in the day, an anonymous note appeared in her faculty mailbox: "You gave the exact same lecture WORD FOR WORD twice this week." It was a student's handwriting—she recognized his oblong Os. No doubt word of Yvonne's forgetfulness had gotten around school and been brought to George's attention as well. Summer school was no longer an option; she'd be lucky to have a job in the fall.

"Mom, please come," Matthew begged during a phone conversation in mid-April when they had little else to discuss. Yvonne had been standing in rain boots on her porch. She would have been flattered by Matthew's invitation if he actually seemed to want her presence, but she knew he was including her for the sake of appearances. If Callie's parents were joining them, how could he explain his mother's absence?

"It looks like Aurelia and Henry are coming now too," he added.

The prospect of Aurelia's presence—and especially Henry's—made the trip more alluring. Yvonne had worried for so long that Aurelia would reject any romantic attention, just as she had shielded herself from her parents' affection. Now Yvonne was quietly thrilled whenever Henry put his arm around Aurelia and Aurelia allowed it to remain.

"Could I come for part of it?" Yvonne asked Matthew.

It had all been settled during that one long phone call.

Once they decided Yvonne would meet Matthew, the Campbells, Aurelia, and Henry halfway through their cruise, in
Turkey, she knew she would spend the preceding week and
two days in Datça. As soon as she made the decision, her
mood improved and the light drizzle ceased. She removed
the take-out menus rubber-banded to her doorknob and
threw them in the trash.

That evening Yvonne had gone online and found this
house. A "gracious house," a "meer walk" from the beach, the
website said. She would spend nine days here and then the
boat would pick her up in the Datça harbor.

In Ali Çelik's kitchen, she continued eating cherries
until her stomach was full and her fingers were purple. She
cleaned up and washed her hands, made sure the door and
windows were locked, and with heavy legs walked up to the
master bedroom.

She changed into her pajamas, brushed her teeth, rinsed
her swollen feet in the shower, and collapsed onto the bed.
The headboard suggested it was king-sized, but as she moved
under the covers toward the center, Yvonne discovered two
mattresses had been pushed together, bound by a single
sheet. At home, she had started sleeping in the middle of her
queen mattress—it made her feel less small, less irrelevant
than staying on her side, or his—but here that would not be
possible. Each night she would have to choose.

She lay on the bed with the light on, staring at a hook in
the ceiling, directly above the bed. It was an eyehook, the
kind used to hang a plant. Who would want to hang a plant

from there?

She couldn't sleep. She stood and scanned the bookshelf. The majority of the books were in Turkish—even *The Da Vinci Code*, whose ubiquitous cover design Yvonne recognized. A few books were in German, and one in English: *The Woman's Guide to Anal Sex*. She read the spine again to make sure she wasn't mistaken. She opened the front cover and an order slip from Amazon.com slipped out. It had been sent to "Manon." Yvonne flipped through the book, pausing at the diagrams, and replaced the slip and the book on the shelf. Çelik apparently hadn't gotten around to putting everything away in time for his renter.

She returned to bed, trying to get comfortable. Various images flew, unbeckoned, to her mind: the note she had found beneath the windshield wiper of her car after Peter's memorial service, which read, "Can't you see what you did? If you had parked your car one foot back someone else could have parked in front of you. But you didn't. Next time, try not to be so selfish. Try to think of other people in this world." The fact that she focused on this note, that week and for the following months—and still, now—was maddening, baffling. A note about her parked car! But it seemed to contain all that she hated about that time, those days of obligation and defeat.

And then there was the image of the woman in the gray winter coat who had appeared at her doorstep all those Decembers ago. Yvonne had been pouring water into the red bowl at the base of the Christmas tree when she saw a woman she didn't recognize walking up their front steps. Even the woman's gait was angry. A loud, determined knock. Yvonne opened the door.

"Are you Aurelia's mother?" the woman said. Her face was ravaged, her eyes wild.

"Yes," Yvonne said.

"Well," the woman said, "I want you to know that your daughter just landed my daughter in intensive care."

How deceived Yvonne had been to believe Aurelia was sober then, that it was so easy to return from a rehab center in Arizona to Burlington High School. How deluded she had been to think that Aurelia wasn't dealing. It was what they had told Yvonne and Peter in the family counseling sessions they'd gone to: "All kids who do drugs, deal drugs." "Not our Aurelia," she said to Peter, who was reluctant to welcome their daughter back home. "Not our Aurelia," he had repeated, but coming out of his mouth, the words meant something very different.

Soon the two episodes joined together, and it was the enraged mother leaving a note on Yvonne's car. Yvonne shook her head, as though she could detach the image from her mind. Her skin was moist, covered with salt. She got up and swung open the window. The wind promptly swept it shut. She looked at the clock. Three. She'd been trying to sleep for two hours. She tried sleeping on her side, with a pillow between her legs, the way she had when she was pregnant. She tried to sleep on her stomach. The pillowcase was rough on her face. She removed a well-worn T-shirt from her suitcase and wrapped it around the pillow.

At dawn she realized the crocheted curtains offered no solace from the light. She rose to examine her other options for sleep. As she stood on the threshold of each of the other bedrooms, she was reminded of her younger self. Every night, after brushing her teeth, she would check on the twins. Matthew's room smelled of buttermilk, that heavy scent of boy. But from the start Aurelia had been a restless sleeper, given to bizarre positionings. One night her legs would be crawling the wall by her bed, her mouth open in amazement. The next she would be facedown, limbs spread like a skydiver.

At six in the morning, wandering the Datça house like a phantom, Yvonne settled on the room with the twin beds and heavy curtains, and crawled into the bed closer to the door. She needed to sleep; she wanted to be strong the next day. It had been twenty-eight years since she and Peter had honeymooned in Datça. She wanted to wake up ready.

A piercing sound was slicing through the house. A siren? An air raid? She rolled out of bed, taking the covers with her at first, then disentangled herself. She ran into the hallway and tried to determine the source. It seemed to be coming from everywhere around her—above, below, the walls themselves. She was surrounded. She ran down the stairs and it shrieked louder. In the living room, she lunged toward something black, plastic, near the TV. A telephone. She listened to it wail again, and heard similar cries coming from above, from what she now realized were the other phones.

She picked up the phone nearest her. How did one say hello in Turkish? She settled on "Allo."

"Good morning. Did I wake you? It's Ali Çelik!"

"I was resting . . ."

"You can't sleep the day away!"

What time was it?

"I was calling to check on you, to make sure everything is okay."

"The house is great," she said, looking around the living room. In the morning, it looked less romantic, more sterile. But still, it was clearly a well-kept, clean house.

"Good. I'd like to come by and say hello."

"Yes," Yvonne said. "And I owe you the remainder of the deposit."

"Oh, yes, that too," Mr. Çelik said, as though it was an afterthought. "Maybe I'll stop by in two hours?"

"Sure," said Yvonne. "What time is it now?"

"Eight o'clock. Time to get up!"

Upstairs, she changed out of her pajamas, which she noticed were threadbare at the thighs and faded everywhere. Peter would have bought her a new set by now. He was the one who pointed out when the heels of her boots were wearing down, he was the one who suggested it was time to trade in her old Toyota. Yvonne, the youngest of three daughters, was not accustomed to shopping for something new when the old, or handed-down, could suffice.

She dressed in a crisp skirt and a bright plum top, and

ran a comb through her hair. A week before the trip, she had been to a hairdresser who, after an hour of snipping and brushing and blow-drying, pronounced Yvonne's cut "youthful." For an hour after leaving the salon, she felt lighter, walking on the balls of her feet until she noticed the heads of every other fifty-something-year-old in Burlington, and even some sixty-year-olds, were similarly coiffed. Now she pulled her hair up behind her head, securing as much of it as would stay into a short ponytail.

She carried her purse with her downstairs to the living room and lay on her back on the blue couch, her hands joined over her chest, her ankles crossed on the armrest. She looked, she thought, like a parody of someone in a psychiatrist's office. But here she could fall asleep and still be able to hear the doorbell when Mr. Çelik arrived.

A thump. Yvonne awoke and leaped up, but no one was at the door. She returned to the couch and saw her unzipped purse had fallen to the floor and some of the contents had spilled. She knelt down on the zebra-skin rug, the coarse hair scratching her shins. Beneath the couch, she saw her tin of lip balm, the squashed orange earplugs she had used on the flight, and the small bottle of evening primrose oil she kept with her when she traveled. The capsules had helped her through menopause, and now she was afraid to be without them.

She slid her arm beneath the couch and swept it left and right, checking to make sure she had found everything. Her wrist brushed against a small tube of toothpaste, also from the plane, and then her hand hit something hard and smooth. She pulled out a large picture frame and turned it over.

Mr. Çelik's wife—Yvonne recognized her from the photos on the refrigerator—was naked, her legs spread, her pubic hair shaved. A large red ribbon had been tied around her breasts, the bow dangling between her nipples. She was holding a sign printed with seven Turkish words. Yvonne couldn't decipher their meaning, but knew from the punctuation that a question was being posed.

Yvonne put the photo back and sat up on the couch. She unscrewed the tin of lip balm and applied it to her mouth with her index finger. A minute later, she applied it again. The night before, a thought had wafted into her mind as she tried to sleep, and she remembered it now. She climbed the stairs to the master bedroom and stood up on the mattress. The ceiling hook was toward the foot of the bed, and she placed a finger through its eye and tugged. It was sturdy enough to hold a few hundred pounds.

She neatened the blanket and climbed to the bedroom on the top floor. Spread out on the bed was the contraption. There had been a scandal at Burlington High two years before involving the girls soccer coach, the captain of the boys lacrosse team, and a sex swing, and though Yvonne had never seen one before, she knew a sex swing was what lay before her now. Why hadn't it been stored away with the naked photo and who knew what else? Why had it been carried upstairs to this room?

A chime echoed dimly: the doorbell. She ran down the

spiral staircase, and when she arrived at the front door she was dizzy, almost panting. She unbolted and unchained and turned the three locks, took a breath, and opened the door.

Mr. Çelik had Mediterranean skin, a small, childlike nose, and thick black hair that had been swept back, as though by a brush or a strong breeze. In front of the house a convertible was parked, its top down. He was young for someone so wealthy.

"You are Yvonne," he said, as if he himself had just christened her.

She smiled. "Yes."

"Welcome to Datça." He extended his arms in the living room, to the kitchen. "You like my house?"

"Very much. It's lovely. How long have you had it?"

"Two years."

"Where do you live?"

"I have another home not too far from here, a home with vineyards. You should come for dinner one night."

She noticed they were still standing in the doorway. "Would you like to come into your house?" she said.

"Please," he said, and made an exaggerated demonstration of wiping his sandals on the doormat. "It's a beautiful day."

Yvonne smiled. She didn't want to let on that she had not been outside. They moved into the dining area and stood by the table.

"I have your money," she said.

"Let's not talk about that yet." He lifted his hand as though to shield himself from the thought of money. "How do you like my Datça?"

"I like it very much. I was actually here before."

"Really? When?"

"Maybe twenty-five years ago," Yvonne said. It had been twenty-eight years exactly.

"You must have liked it, no, if you come back?"

"I was on my honeymoon," she said.

"Oh, yes, everyone has fun on their honeymoon."

Yvonne looked at the floor, embarrassed. She thought of the sex swing and the photo, and the parts either might have played in *his* honeymoon.

"And is your husband joining you?"

"No," Yvonne said. "He passed away." Up until a year ago she had told people Peter had been killed. But when they realized no knives or guns or poison had been involved, they seemed less interested, even disappointed, and this inevitably turned Yvonne against them. There had been a long period when the details of his death were the only thing on her mind at any given time of day, and always at night.

"I am sorry," Mr. Çelik said. "I'm so sorry." His sympathy, so unexpected from a stranger, caused a stinging sensation in her nose, the start of tears.

"It's okay," she said, as though consoling him. Now he was the one looking at the floor.

"Maybe," she started, unsure of what she was going to say. She had to save him. "Maybe you could give me some good restaurant recommendations? It's been so long."

"Of course," he said, brightening up. She knew his type,

the kind of person who was happiest with a task, a purpose. "I will draw you a map."

They both looked around for paper. "Maybe in that cabinet there," Mr. Çelik said. "Do you mind if I look?"

He located a pad of paper with thin blue lines spaced widely, and sketched a small map. "Here we are," he said, and drew a star, "and here's a good place for meat, and here"—he squiggled another star—"is a good place for fish." The watch on his wrist was large and thick black hair sprouted up on either side of the wide band. "Tell them you're staying at my house."

"Thank you," she said, taking the drawing from him. She already knew the tangle of crooked lines and wayward stars would prove useless.

She lifted her purse and, this time, Mr. Çelik did not object. She removed the white envelope she'd been given by the woman with the plastic thimble on her thumb who exchanged her money at the Amsterdam airport. Mr. Çelik had specified in his e-mail that he preferred to be paid in euros rather than Turkish lire, but she confirmed with him now.

"Euros, yes?" she said.

"Yes, better than lire. I have more faith in their economy."

"But I changed money into lire too. Around town, can I use lire or . . . ?"

"Lire are fine, but secretly everyone prefers euros."

"Good to know," she said, and counted out the bills slowly on the dining room table. When she was through, Mr. Çelik counted them again quickly before stacking them. He was clearly a man accustomed to dealing with cash.

"Next time I see you I'll bring you a receipt."

"When will that be?" Yvonne said, hoping she didn't sound desperate. It was only now, upon his imminent departure, that she fully comprehended the solitary existence that lay before her. When she had been in Burlington, surrounded by people who paid too much attention to her social schedule, or the paucity of it, isolation had seemed the perfect antidote. But now, only the morning after her arrival in Datça, she was beginning to have her doubts.

"I'll check in," Mr. Çelik said as he started for the door. Was it her imagination or, now that he had his money, was he no longer looking at her?

"Oh," he said, turning around.

"Yes?"

He gave her body the cursory glance people gave to the shapes of the elderly. She no longer had a body or a figure; she had a shape.

"What days are good for the maid?"

"Maid?" She had never used a maid at home.

"Yes, it's included in the rental. Two maid visits during your stay."

"Wednesday?" She wasn't sure what day it was. "And Saturday."

"Good," he said. "I will tell her. And not too early. I know you like to sleep."

Yvonne smiled and stood with one hand on the door as

he stepped outside. They nodded at each other and then he turned. She watched his calves as he walked down the stairs.

She was suddenly ravenous. She opened the refrigerator again, as though something inside might have materialized with the arrival of morning. Nothing but cherries, now looking worse than they had the night before. She would walk to town, eat, buy groceries, and take a stroll along the beach. She hid half of her remaining euros in the pocket of a woman's raincoat she found hanging in the master bedroom closet. Then she gathered her things—straw hat, purse, the ring of house keys, which included a heavy charm in the shape of a boat.

Outside, the sun was so strong she imagined she could see its rays, thin and sharp as blades. Yvonne turned left at the first street that sloped downhill, looking for a street sign to help her find her way back, but there wasn't even a lamppost in sight. Nor were there sidewalks. She kept to the edge of the road and passed chickens and a family of turkeys. *Turkeys in Turkey*, she said to herself, and was briefly amused until the animals strutted closer and she saw they were scrawny, filthy creatures. She would remember them at Thanksgiving.

Yellow houses, both crumbling and remodeled, stood clustered together, their red-tiled roofs industrial and depressing. The windows of vacant-looking buildings bore signs that said SATILIK in red, with a phone number, while the windowsills of visibly occupied houses were lined with unflowering plants potted in large yogurt containers. Between the houses sat acres of desiccated land that had not yet been developed save for failed attempts to grow grapes. The rows of vines had shriveled, leaving only wooden posts.

From somewhere below came the call to prayer. The sound was fuzzy, as though being broadcast through a megaphone on a parade float.

When she and Peter had first arrived in Turkey they spent a night in Istanbul at a hotel with a view of the Blue Mosque. At four in the morning, Yvonne was awoken by what sounded like a man singing beneath their window. "Can you ask him to keep it down?" she had mumbled to Peter, and he, jet-lagged, had obliged. Through half-closed eyes she saw his gray shape move to the window, and then she heard him laugh.

"It's the call to prayer," he said. He crawled back into bed and, unable to fall back to sleep given their proximity to the mosque, they made love, their limbs beating at the tangle of the comforter and sheets, like swimmers struggling not to drown.

She had not remembered this until now. *Good*, she thought. It was happening. After Peter's death, she had cocooned herself in a mood, both woolly and ethereal, that had separated her from her kids, her students, from the rest of the world. But it was good to remember these things. Already the sky and the ocean felt closer, their colors brighter. She realized she had stopped walking. *You can remember and move at the same time*, she said to herself. Careful not to slip in her sandals, she continued down the crooked blocks until she reached the main street. Swerving mopeds and small honking cars crowded the road. The sidewalks were narrow and filled with tables where shirtless old men played checkers. Outside Internet cafés, teenage boys sold phone cards. Yvonne passed a store where rolled-up rugs, standing erect as columns on either side of the entranceway, emitted a musty scent in the heat.

She crossed the road, quickening her pace as she approached the water. This was where she and Peter had spent most of their nights. They had walked along the promenade and, each evening, permitted a different maître d' to beckon them to eat at his establishment. Always they sat at an outside table and watched the sunset stretch wide and narrow across the flat sea.

Now, as she started down the length of the promenade, hope swelled in Yvonne's chest. Hope that this would be the reward for her trip: she would feel the way she felt during their honeymoon, she would remember every conversation, every joke, every breeze, every laugh and silence, and the feel of Peter's thigh, warm from the sun, against hers. She felt she was tracing an unraveled ball of string to its source. They had been so happy at the beginning.

The beach was filthy. Small plastic bags, gelatinous in the sun, had been deposited by the tide on the wet sand. Dark, dead leaves swirled and settled around a boat that looked like it had docked on the beach five years before and never left. The water too looked dirty, the foam of the small waves that crashed on the beach the color of beer. The promenade itself was not half as populated as she remembered it. The short trees bordering the walkway provided little shade and had rooted themselves under the cement, creating small hills and crevices. From somewhere in the trees came the eerie day-time hooting of owls.

Half the restaurants had been shut down. The remaining ones displayed sick-looking fish on beds of crushed gray ice. With soiled rags, waiters shooed away mangy cats trolling for food. A sprinkling of tourists speaking German sat outside the cafés, their skin sunburned to a peculiar shade of orange.

In the distance, she saw the waterfront hotel where she and Peter had stayed. As she approached the building she noticed the balconies were bare—no smokers, no beach towels draped over railings to dry. Closer now, she saw broken windows, an overgrown lawn, a drained pool, the light blue paint at its bottom blistered and cracked.

She looked around for food and a place to sit. In front of the abandoned hotel, by the water, stood a small ice cream parlor with an outdoor patio that overlooked the dinghies rocking back and forth. Yvonne surveyed the flavors and pointed to pistachio and raspberry. The man behind the counter, his arms spotted with white freckles, scooped her choices into a large glass bowl, and handed her a spoon with a tiny, useless napkin.

She sat at a table and prepared herself to enjoy the coolness, but all she could taste, a moment after swallowing, was the metallic flavor of the spoon. It tasted like other people's mouths, a century of tongues. She put the spoon down and watched the ice cream melt.

For a year after Peter's death, she had wondered how anyone could speak of anything else. When Matthew came to her door six months later—making the long drive from New York in only a few hours—and told her Callie had proposed to him, she thought, *How can you talk about weddings?* "That is the best news, Matthew," she'd said. "You and Callie are a perfect pair." Aurelia called eight months after the funeral to say she'd been sober two years; she'd just gotten her second gold chip at that afternoon's AA meeting. "Oh my darling," Yvonne had said. "I couldn't be more proud." Yvonne *was* proud, but confused, and then confused about why she was confused. How had Aurelia, who had once turned to drinking with any minor provocation, remained sober after her father's death? She didn't want her children to fall apart, but neither did she want them seeming stronger. Was it too much to ask them to stagger around a few more months? No. Such thoughts she couldn't express, not out loud.

It was best that she was here alone. Here she could remember how she was when she wasn't twisted up and selfish. Here, with Peter, she had been generous and world-welcoming. Here, with Peter, everything had been lovely. The promenade was lovely. The water was lovely. The food was lovely. The rain, the feral cats, the keys to their hotel that they'd lost and looked for all day—it was all lovely.

But this place, now, was not lovely. She had expected more of her Datça, their Datça. Wasn't Turkey the home of

Troy and Ephesus? A land where archaeologists came and were startled to find entire towns as they once were? But Datça had not been preserved. It had been looted by tide and tourists and the scalding sun that robbed boats of their color. It was now a destination spot for Italians and Hungarians who had been deceived by unknowledgeable travel agents. Even the Brits in Marmaris didn't make it this far; they knew better.

She walked back up the hill. A black dog turned a corner and sprinted toward her. Three men were trailing the animal, yelling, and Yvonne was nearly toppled as a fourth man joined the chase. He captured the dog. It was a big dog, Yvonne thought, until she saw it was a goat. The four men circled the poor animal, holding him captive. When Yvonne reached the top of the block, she turned to see the goat being slung over one of the men's shoulders. The animal's front and back legs were tied together with rope and his head turned left and right, as though in disbelief.

Yvonne was breathing heavily by the time she got to her street. Her face pulsed with heat, and she felt sweat trickling down the back of her thighs. The hem of her skirt seemed to wipe at it with each step. The website listing had claimed the house was only five hundred meters from the ocean, but this too had been an untruth.

She paused outside the house and squinted. A woman was standing at the door.

"Hello?" Yvonne said as she climbed the stairs.

"Hello," said the woman. She was slight, striking, with

straight brown hair that fell below her shoulders.

"Can I help you?" Yvonne asked as she reached the patio.

"I am Ali Çelik's wife. Özlem."

"I'm Yvonne. Nice to meet you." Yvonne extended her hand. Özlem's grasp was bird-like. She smiled tentatively, revealing a narrow but not unattractive gap between her front teeth.

Özlem stared directly at Yvonne, with a look that suggested she was trying to determine something about her. But what? Whether she was wealthy? Whether she had once been pretty?

"Please," Yvonne said, holding open the door. "Come in."

Özlem stepped inside tentatively. She had round hazel eyes that looked into Yvonne's and begged *please*.

"Would you like to sit down, Özlem?" Yvonne offered, gesturing toward the living room.

"Thank you," Özlem said.

She was wearing a sheer fuchsia blouse, tight jeans that narrowed at the ankles, and high heels with pointed toes. Her outfit seemed better suited for a nightclub than a casual visit to a beach home. Yvonne asked if she'd like something to drink—tea? Özlem placed her hands together, as though to applaud the idea.

In the kitchen, Yvonne placed the kettle on the stove. She removed a small carton of cream from the refrigerator, and as she closed the door she glanced at the photo of Ali Çelik on the boat. Then she looked closer. She studied the woman with her arm around his waist. The woman had the same color hair as the guest currently seated in the living room, but her nose was straighter, her eyes almond-shaped and not round. The woman was not Özlem.

The kettle began to hiss, the prelude to a whistle, and Yvonne turned off the flame. She floated the tea bags in two mugs and placed the mugs and sugar and cream on a tray.

Yvonne knew now that Özlem was not the woman on the refrigerator, and not the woman in the photo beneath the couch. She returned to the living room to find Özlem sitting upright, looking around with the curiosity of a first-time visitor.

"Thank you," Özlem said as Yvonne placed the tray on the coffee table in front of her.

"Tea and sugar," Yvonne said, and smiled at her own joke, a joke Özlem did not get.

"My husband told me about your husband," Özlem said. "I am sorry."

"Thank you," Yvonne said, and then felt foolish to have thanked her. But it was a relief to not have to tell the story again.

"So you are alone here?"

"Yes. And then I'll meet my son in a week. My son and his fiancée. And my daughter and her boyfriend."

Özlem nodded, as though to dismiss her own question.

"How long have you and Mister—how long have you and Ali been married?" Yvonne was testing Özlem, still deciding if she was a deluded ex-wife or a fibbing lover.

"Well, we were married five years, and now I don't

know . . . do you mind if I smoke?"

"Fine," Yvonne said. Aurelia had started smoking when she'd stopped drinking the first time, at sixteen, and Yvonne had grown used to it.

Özlem tried three times to get her cigarette to light, swearing in Turkish each time it didn't. Finally successful, she inhaled deeply and threw back her head. She was a beautiful woman.

"We were married for five years and then I decided I wanted a divorce."

Yvonne nodded. Teaching had taught her to be a good listener. She had learned not to say *Yes* or *Excuse me?* or express any surprise. She had discovered people felt most free to say what was on their minds when Yvonne bobbed her chin up and down encouragingly.

"And so he took a girlfriend," Özlem said. "This is the girlfriend's house."

Yvonne tried not to increase the range of her nodding. She kept it consistent, a metronome.

Özlem took another drag of her cigarette. It was unclear whether she was going to speak again.

"And what happened to the girlfriend?" Yvonne asked.

"What do you mean?"

"I mean where did she go? She's not here," Yvonne said, and gestured around the room with her eyes.

"Her mother is ill. She returned to Paris for two months."

"And then you came back here?"

"Ali thought it was a good time for us to see if we are able to work things out."

Yvonne nodded. Özlem's story added up.

"Ali bought her this house," Özlem said, looking around with a mixture of distaste and awe.

"Why did she need her own house?"

"She didn't. It was one of his grand gestures. He bought me a house when we met. And I can imagine she probably did not so much like being in that house. All my things are there. Even when I went back to Istanbul for a while, when I was considering a separation, I left everything in the house."

Yvonne watched Özlem's cigarette. It was balanced on the ashtray, the ashes about to drop to the table.

"Why did you want a separation?" Yvonne knew she was violating her own rule, but she was curious, and Özlem didn't seem shy.

Özlem took a drag of the cigarette and the ashes fell on her jeans. She brushed them off, annoyed. Then she looked Yvonne in the eye. "He hit me," she said.

"Oh dear," Yvonne said, though something about the way Özlem said this disturbed Yvonne on another level. "Oh my dear. I'm so sorry."

Now it was Özlem who nodded, accepting the sympathy. "So I left," she said. "I went to Istanbul and I tried to be a single again. I tried to pursue the career I had when Ali and I met."

"What was that?"

"I was a face of Dove."

"Pardon?"

"You know Dove?"

"No."

"The soap?"

"Oh, yes, the soap."

"I was one of the faces of Dove."

"That's great," Yvonne said. For the first time, she thought she saw Özlem smile a happy smile. "Have you always been a model?"

"No. I studied at a hotel and restaurant management school in Switzerland. But I hated it. I went because it was the occasion to live abroad. But I knew I didn't want to work in the travel industry."

"I can see that," Yvonne said. It was hard enough for her to watch students pass through her classroom each year. She couldn't imagine getting to know guests only for a week, or even just a night.

"I didn't want to spend my life working for other people. To be sweet and nice even if they are terrible people. That's not easy for me."

"But you learned English at the school?"

"Yes, I'm a fast learner," she said with the complete immodesty Yvonne had frequently observed in people speaking in their non-native language.

Özlem took out another cigarette, and then, as though recalling that she had just finished one, put it back in its box. Merit Lights.

"So, how did you start modeling?" Yvonne said.

"It was so funny. I just come back from Switzerland and

I was in a shopping mall with a girlfriend of mine. I was trying to buy makeup and the woman at the makeup place said maybe I want to have something to cover my freckles. I got upset because my whole life people have been making me feel bad about my freckles. So I am walking through the mall, very upset, and a man comes up to my friend and me and says he would very much like to make my photograph. I ask him what for, and he says he is looking for people for the campaign of Dove. So he makes my photo, and I feel better, but I don't think anything will happen, do you know? It is rare when things actually happen."

"I guess that's true," Yvonne said, trying to decide if it was.

"But then a few days later, I get a call asking me to come in for a photo session. It was so much fun. They dress me up, and give me lots of champagne to drink, and there are many people telling me how beautiful I am. 'Oh, you are so beautiful. Beauty, yes, you.' It was a great day. And then a week later they tell me they want me to be in the campaign of Dove in Turkey. They want me to be the freckle girl."

"The freckle girl?"

"In every country—Saudi Arabia, Kuwait—they have one girl in the campaign who has freckles."

Yvonne tilted her head the way she did when she was trying to understand something.

"Because underneath my picture it says 'I have freckles, but I'm still beautiful.'"

"Freckles aren't beautiful here?"

"No, here they're ugly. Is it not that way in America?"

"No," Yvonne said. "No." She looked closer at Özlem's face. "But you don't have that many freckles!" She counted maybe five on each cheek.

"I do, but I don't care anymore, because they are what got me a job. I was on billboards all over the country, and when you buy a soap, a Dove soap, my picture is in the pamphlet."

"I'll have to go look," Yvonne said, gesturing her chin toward the stairs.

"I am doubtful there's any soap in this house. I am doubtful she allows Dove soap here!" She scoffed theatrically.

Özlem's face turned toward the window. "It was the first campaign I did and then I met Ali. It was so funny. He saw the billboard. Everyone saw the billboard—it was all over. And he came up to me at a club in Istanbul one night, a very nice club—he was there with some business people—and he said, 'You have freckles, but I still think you're beautiful.'"

Özlem laughed. She looked five years younger when she laughed. Yvonne guessed she was twenty-eight or twenty-nine.

"And then you moved to Datça?"

"We dated for a while, and then he asked me to marry him. And then, yes, we moved down here. I was never happy here, though. I don't like this town. I like my house and the vineyard, and we don't really need to leave it, but I don't like this town." She looked at Yvonne. "Sorry," she said.

"It's okay," said Yvonne. "I don't like it either."

They both laughed.

"So are you sad you came here? Maybe you regret not going somewhere nicer?"

"No, I don't regret it," Yvonne said. "I've been here before. Many years ago."

Özlem nodded, as though she knew this. "You must have liked it if you come back."

"I did. I liked it very much. It was different then too."

"That's what everybody says. It used to be better." Özlem picked an invisible piece of something off her jeans. "Do you mind if I ask you a personal question?"

Yvonne paused. "Okay."

"What do you plan to do all day?"

Yvonne laughed. "I want to remember."

"You want to remember your honeymoon?" Ali must have told her.

"I guess the honeymoon. I just want to remember him, the days we spent here. We lived in the same house for twenty-six years and sometimes when I'm home, walking through the rooms, I think, 'Did he take the splinter out of my daughter's foot, or was it *my* foot?' I'll think, 'Did we go through a phase where we listened to this record for a year, or was it that record?' Everything gets jumbled. Too many things happened in each of those rooms, on the stairway, in the garden. And I can't ask him."

"Did you have a good marriage?" Özlem asked.

Yvonne nodded. She had decided long ago that it had been good. And after his death, it felt unnecessary to question the storyline. They had met in a fantastically romantic way. They had beautiful twins together. They lived comfortably in the comfortable state of Vermont, they had good teaching jobs at the same high school, they traveled well together, and often. If you excluded Aurelia, as Peter often had, things had been perfect, hadn't they?

"How long you are together?"

"We were going to celebrate our twenty-sixth anniversary when he died."

"You celebrate twenty-six?"

"We never had a twenty-fifth anniversary because our daughter was going through a tough time, so we were going to celebrate our twenty-sixth—"

"With a party?"

"Yes."

"A big one?" Özlem asked. She seemed like someone who would be fond of festive occasions.

"Sort of. We aren't big on parties. I mean we never were—except for our kids' birthdays, of course. But for our anniversary, we were going to invite my sisters in New Mexico, and our friends from all over, and have a big party in the backyard. We were going to have a piñata and . . ." Yvonne couldn't recall the other plans they had made. All the details—the music, the guest list, the food—had been subsumed by funeral arrangements.

"That sounds fun," said Özlem, rescuing her from trying to remember.

"It would have been, yes." Yvonne smiled. She had experienced a strange sensation, though, a week after his death, or maybe sooner: relief that she would not have to plan and put on this party. She could not admit the relief, just as she could not admit that she took a tiny bit of pleasure in the newness of certain things—of eating breakfast food for dinner, of shoveling the snow on the front steps herself, of not having to talk about Aurelia with Peter, of not having to avoid talking about Aurelia with Peter. But at the two-year mark even the new had turned old, and the realization had settled in, like the creak of a floorboard that never goes away, that she was, in fact, a widow. No, the realization was not a floorboard. It was a house. The grief fell in on her like a house collapsing.

"I hope I didn't upset you," Özlem said, and leaned her hands forward. They were slender hands, with large but tasteful rings on three fingers.

"No," said Yvonne. "No."

"I'd like to come see you again, if that is all right."

"Yes, of course."

"Maybe tomorrow?"

Yvonne nodded. She was pleased Özlem seemed to have taken to her as quickly as she had taken to Özlem.

"Is it strange being in this house?" Yvonne asked while walking her to the door.

"A little," Özlem said without hesitating. "Maybe next time, you'll give a tour for me?"

"Sure," Yvonne said, briefly wondering if it was the house, not Yvonne, that interested Özlem.

They kissed good-bye on both cheeks, and Yvonne closed the door. She brought their cups to the sink, cleaned them, set them upside down to dry, and went outside to the patio with a magazine she'd brought on the flight. She tried to follow the words on the page, but couldn't concentrate. Something about Özlem's visit nagged at the back of her head, and hunger sounded in her stomach.

She had no desire to return to Datça's promenade, to its restaurants, so she took the car and drove until she found a grocery store. She stocked up on food she would have been able to find in Burlington, but never ate at home: Nutella, granola cereal, pomegranates, olives, small apples, frozen pizzas, and a pint of ice cream with nuts.

Back at the house, she ate her pizza on the patio, and watched a young couple with suitcases walking up and down the street, studying the numbers on houses and consulting a piece of paper. After a few minutes, they must have decided they were in the wrong place altogether. They placed their luggage in the trunk of a car and drove away.

After dinner, Yvonne quickly grew tired. As she drifted off to sleep in the room with the twin beds, she knew what it was that had been disturbing her. When Özlem said Ali hit her, she had a challenging expression on her face and her eyes said, *What, you don't believe me?* It was a frequent expression of Aurelia's, used both when she was lying and when she was telling the truth.

The first time Yvonne had picked her up at the police station—there had been two times—Aurelia had dared her mother to doubt her story. "You really think I would have gone out of my way to steal those earrings? Did you *see* those earrings? They're the kind of thing Becca would wear." Becca was Matthew's girlfriend at the time—a doe-eyed girl who wore pink pants and pearls with sweatshirts. She embodied everything Aurelia claimed to hate, though Yvonne suspected she was secretly jealous another girl had stolen Matthew's attention, his help with homework, his rides to school. "Really, Mom. *Think* about it."

Yvonne was awoken by the sound of people in the house below. Something falling to the floor. A man's voice. A woman's voice.

It was already light out. Yvonne walked downstairs. "Hello?" she called out. She heard more voices. In the living room, a man and a boy were sitting on the couch, watching television.

"Can I help you?" she said. The boy looked at her. A lock of hair, the shape of a comma, bisected his forehead. The man called for someone else, and for a moment Yvonne felt scared. What if there was a team of burglars? But what had they broken in for? To watch TV?

A woman emerged from the kitchen wearing a head scarf and carrying a broom. When she smiled at Yvonne, her sadness was made more profound. She mimed sweeping and scrubbing. Of course, the maid. It must be Wednesday.

"Oh, hello," Yvonne said. She wanted to take the broom from the woman and tell her to go home. Yvonne had been in the house for less than thirty-six hours, and had left little trace of being there. But she worried that if she did ask the maid to leave, it would mean she wouldn't work, and wouldn't be paid by Mr. Çelik.

The boy was standing at the edge of the living room, peering at Yvonne with parted lips.

"Hello," she said.

"Hello," he said, and giggled. "Where you?" he said.

"Where am I from?" Yvonne asked.

The boy didn't say anything.

"America."

The boy smiled.

"Vermont."

The boy's face was blank.

"Let me show you," Yvonne said. She stepped into the living room and retrieved an atlas she had seen on the bookshelf. The boy's father was watching what looked like a danceathon on TV.

The atlas opened to Turkey. She searched for the peninsula in the southwest corner of the country. Datça was a small black dot on the farthest edge, at the point where the Mediterranean and the Aegean came together.

She turned the pages until she got to the United States, and showed the boy Vermont. She was always surprised by how far away she now lived from New Mexico, where she had been raised. The boy studied the map with great seriousness and carried it to his father, who glanced at the image and then said something stern to the boy. Yvonne knew he was instructing the boy not to bother her, and she didn't know how to tell the father it was okay, that it was the simple company of kids she now missed. That it was her children's childhoods she missed. The boy sat down on the couch, his legs straight out, and picked at a scab on his elbow. From the kitchen came the clank of dishes being washed by hand.

Yvonne knew she needed to leave. She felt uncomfortable letting the woman clean a clean house, and she felt more uncomfortable watching the man watch TV while his wife scrubbed and mopped and did whatever else she was going to do.

Yvonne retreated to the bedroom and changed into her new swimsuit. In the catalogue, the one-piece had appeared to be an innocuously pale yellow. But the package had arrived at her door two days before her trip—too late to be exchanged—and the swimsuit had turned out to be the pungent yellow of a yield sign. She called her next-door neighbor, Anita, and asked her to come over so she could get her opinion. Anita, who was wearing a hat rimmed with flowers, had pronounced the suit "fun."

Fun, Yvonne repeated to herself as she stood in front of the mirror in Datça, tightening the straps, lifting the suit higher on her chest. She pulled on a shapeless turquoise sundress Aurelia had dubbed her "missionary attire," packed a bag, and set off in the car with no destination in mind. She drove down the hill to the main road with the air-conditioning on high and the windows down low. Despite the maid, or perhaps in part because she had escaped from witnessing the maid, Yvonne was in good spirits. Upon further consideration, she attributed the bulk of this feeling to her conversation with Özlem. While she suspected Özlem of lying to her about being hit, this only made her more intriguing. Özlem was not Yvonne's problem to solve, and so she could listen, gasp, advise—all without having to watch the consequences unfold.

Since Peter's death, Yvonne had come to value friendship more than romance. On the phone with old classmates, she asked probing questions, far more curious about her friends' jobs and children than she'd ever been before. But Yvonne was certain she wouldn't love again—not a man, not sexually. She couldn't picture a man other than Peter lying next to her at night. It seemed as natural as sleeping next to a bear. Nor could she imagine adjusting to the feel of another man's thumb on her nipple, those particular pink marks etched onto his skin by the waistband of his underwear, the frequency of how often he rose in the night to pee.

Seventeen months after Peter's death, she had agreed to go on a date set up by a woman who owned the neighborhood health-food store. This was the same woman who had told Yvonne about a website that e-mailed subscribers a new vocabulary word every morning, and Yvonne had signed up for the service because it was free, and she liked the non-surprise of its arrival in her inbox. She could never be sure what any other e-mail might say, which long-lost friends or colleagues would have only just learned of Peter's passing, and written to offer their condolences, their platitudes. But the word of the day was uncomplicated in its anonymity and consistency.

Edward had seemed promising: a former mayor of a small town, he had broad shoulders and hair that appeared to always have just been washed. Yvonne soon understood that Edward was also a subscriber to the word-of-the-day e-mail, most likely at the store owner's prompting as well. Each time they had gone out together—to a Sunday brunch, to dinner, to a graduation ceremony for Seeing Eye dogs for the blind (his daughter was an instructor at the school)—he had incorporated a recent word-of-the-day into his conversation. At first Yvonne thought he was kidding, gently mocking their mutual friend. But he was not kidding. By the third date, Yvonne's elbows locked into her side in agitated anticipation as she listened to him steer the conversation in a direction that would allow him to incorporate *pleonexia*. At a bus stop bench she sat him down. "Whatever is happening between us is fugacious," she told him, knowing he would understand. It was Saturday, and *fugacious* had been Thursday's word.

When Yvonne reached the main road, she drove out of Datça without knowing the speed limit, or how fast she was going. She didn't care to convert kilometers to miles, just as she didn't want to convert the temperature, digitally provided in Celsius on the Renault's control panel, to Fahrenheit.

Rather quickly, the stations on the Renault's radio began to fade to static. All except one that broadcast a woman telling jokes in Turkish, each joke punctuated by a laugh track. She told a joke every minute, and the laughter lasted for six seconds, never more, never less. It made Yvonne happy to hear the laughter, as perfunctory as it was. Other people's happiness pleased her, now more than ever. Why?

She sped past gas stations—so many gas stations, each with its owner's name printed at the bottom of the list of prices for diesel, prices for premium gas. She drove past olive trees, sleeping cows, and roadside stands displaying row upon row of porcelain swans, their beaks all turned in the direction of the sun.

She was slowed by trucks doing roadwork ahead, and from the burn in her nostrils she surmised they were pouring tar. As she trailed a slow line of cars, she grew increasingly impatient. At an intersection a small sign caught her eye. KNIDOS 35 KILOMETERS, it said, with an arrow pointing to the left. She turned.

Knidos. She had not known it was so close. She remembered the name, would always remember it. *Knidos* was penciled onto the back of the photo Peter had taken of her there on the last day of their honeymoon. In the photo she was smiling in front of an ancient white amphitheater, wearing a sundress patterned with halved pomegranates. Peter had the photo framed and propped on his desk for his entire career at the high school, and not a semester passed without him telling her a fellow teacher had commented on Yvonne's beauty, her youth, on the way the photo had captured something they hadn't seen before, but now could not believe had escaped their notice.

For the first fifteen minutes of the drive to Knidos, Yvonne wound up a hill, the top of which she could not see.

She felt dwarfed by the mountains around her, which were spotted with short trees at their base, dotted with white rocks in their middle, and bald at their peaks.

Soon the road grew curvier and Yvonne seemed to be emerging above the surrounding mountains. She passed roadside stalls where village women sold honey and almonds. The women wore scarves around their heads, and had thick walking sticks by their sides. Yvonne stopped the car to allow a woman to amble across the road. The woman was bent at the hips, her back horizontal, her cane short. Yvonne would have bought anything from her, but the woman had nothing to sell.

YAKAKÖY said a sign, and a minute later, Yvonne was in the heart of the village. The road turned narrow and bumpy, lined on either side with crumbling and gray buildings that had once been white. Aging men in baseball hats stood in the shade of a bar, watching as she passed. Donkeys seemed to squeeze her car from either side, and the old women gathered in front of the town's two deteriorating mosques narrowed the road further. Yvonne drove slowly, the tires of the Renault barely turning, and when she was released from the claustrophobia of the town she picked up speed.

The landscape was more rugged now, the hills whiter with rock. She felt she was approaching something wondrous. *Any minute now*, she thought, and there it was suddenly spread below her: the Aegean, gleaming in the sun. The road descended and she paused at a turn and looked down on Knidos. The land itself had an hourglass shape, and, where it narrowed at the middle, a harbor had formed on each side. One harbor was empty except for a small fishing boat. The other was wide, majestic; eight or nine yachts docked there, all with tall white masts bearing flags. As she watched, a wooden boat glided in smoothly, like a prop being pulled by invisible strings across a stage. On the radio, the laughter continued.

The road ended at a lot where only six other cars were parked—most people arrived at Knidos by small boats descended from larger boats. As Yvonne stepped out of the car, she was relieved to feel a light wind quivering through the heat; she was pleased she would be spending the day here rather than in Datça. More than pleased, she was proud of herself for coming here, proud of the road for leading her here. Knidos contained all the beauty of worlds old and new.

There was the amphitheater, facing the harbor. She had taught Ancient Civilizations for two years, and now she imagined performances and staged battles taking place on the water. She walked past a restaurant—the only building in Knidos—where waiters pushed open large umbrellas, as though offering them to the sun. Above her, among the ruins, she could make out visitors posing for photos. Yvonne made her way to the beach and then she was alone.

She stretched out her faded towel, its texture rough from having dried on a clothesline. The boats in the harbor were bigger and more beautiful than the ones docked in Datça. Many had two masts and sharp bows, their wood polished and smooth, simultaneously golden and dark. Each bore a different flag: Turkish, Italian, German, French, and one Yvonne couldn't readily identify—Montenegro?

The vessels were close enough to shore that she could make out passengers on the decks with their bikinis and magazines and dark tans—nothing like the orange shades of skin in Datça. At the boats' sterns, fully dressed women were busy setting tables with plates, glasses, and utensils that reflected silver-white light in the sun. It was approaching lunchtime.

The sea made a sound like breath, inhaling and exhaling steadily. Yvonne stood, removed her sundress, dipped one heel in the water, and then carefully molded her feet over the rocks and the moss until she was waist-deep in the ocean. The temperature was perfect, cool enough to wash away the heat of the day. She dove in with her eyes closed and swam for a few strokes before flipping onto her back and then to her side. The salt content was so high that she felt the ocean was ejecting her, as though she would soon rise above it.

She splashed the water away and watched the ripples. It seemed it had been months, years, since she had left a trace of herself in this world. A grief counselor Matthew had sent to her home (in lieu of coming himself, it seemed) had accused her of trying to be invisible. "You seem to want to cease to exist too," the woman said, just before Yvonne asked her to leave.

Yvonne plunged in deeper and swam for as long as her breath would hold. When she emerged, she saw she had traveled closer to one of the boats with a Turkish flag. She could hear voices calling to each other from one end of the boat to the other, and then in her direction.

A woman with a bright white scarf tied around her head was clipping laundry to a line on the side of the boat. She addressed Yvonne, first in Turkish, then in English.

"How feels the water?"

"Refreshing," Yvonne shouted back.

"What do you say?" said the woman.

"It's nice," Yvonne said, and the woman nodded, as though this was something she already knew.

"Where are you from?" said the woman. She was wearing a white blouse tucked into long white shorts, her waist circled by a dark blue belt.

"United States," Yvonne said as she swam closer to the boat. Swimming and shouting at the same time was exhausting. She switched to the breaststroke so she could speak more easily.

"Where in the U.S.?" said the woman. She pronounced the letters *U* and *S* carefully, as though spelling a word for a child.

"Near New York," Yvonne said. She was tired of explaining Vermont.

"Oh," said the woman. "I was near to there. My daughter, she lives in Vermont."

"That's where I'm from!" said Yvonne. It was strangely welcoming to find a woman hanging laundry on the other side of the world who knew something about where Yvonne lived. She felt as though the woman could picture the mismatched greens of Yvonne's living room couch and chairs, the coatrack that stood in her entryway like a leafless tree.

"Please," said the woman, "you must come on the boat. Please, I invite you to have a glass of tea with ice."

Yvonne had no choice but to accept. What would be her excuse not to? That someone was waiting for her on the beach? Once she returned to her towel, she would be alone, as the woman in white would be able to see.

Yvonne swam to the boat. The aluminum ladder was warm on her hands, and Yvonne could hear the water dripping from her swimsuit onto the rungs as she lifted herself up. The woman was waiting for her, a plush white towel in her hands, and she wrapped it around Yvonne as if she were a champion swimmer finishing a record-breaking heat. From afar the woman's trim figure had lent her the air of someone much younger, but up close Yvonne saw that she could be sixty-five, maybe seventy.

"Thank you," Yvonne said. Now that she was out of the water, she tasted the salt on her lips.

"I am Deniz," said the woman. Her teeth were the texture of wood, but her eyes were wet and bright.

"Deniz, I am Yvonne."

They smiled at each other. Yvonne liked her immediately.

"Please, I introduce you to my husband," Deniz said. "Galip." Galip was standing by a table at the stern of the boat, pouring iced tea from a pitcher into a glass. He had a thick gray beard and wore a black bandanna around his bushy hair. His wrinkled white linen shirt was unbuttoned halfway down his chest, and his white shorts reached his knees. He was a stout man with powerful legs, and seemed aware of his fitness, his roguish appeal. A pair of Oakley sunglasses hung around his neck.

"Nice to meet you," said Yvonne.

Galip nodded and handed her the glass of iced tea. It was clear he did not understand English.

"Please, sit down," Deniz said.

"I don't want to interrupt your lunch."

"You don't. Captain Galip eats in one hour. I don't eat after twelve," said Deniz. She paused, waiting for Yvonne to comment. She clarified: "We do boat charter all year and I cook very good food. So I don't like to get fat, I stop eat at twelve."

Two crewmen, no more than eighteen years old and also dressed in white, appeared behind Deniz. She turned to them and barked something in Turkish. Her voice was suddenly unpleasant, the consonants of her words scraping against each other like a zipper. The boys scampered toward the front of the boat.

Deniz turned back to Yvonne and smiled sweetly but without apology. "Where you live in Vermont?"

"Burlington," Yvonne said.

"I see," Deniz said. "My daughter, she live in the capital."

"Montpelier."

Deniz nodded. "She marries a doctor for the back."

"A chiropractor?"

"Yes. He is a nice man. He needs to give me a grandson or

granddaughter—I don't care what it is. He just needs to give me one. Do you have a family?" She had a habit of smiling at the end of each question.

"I have two children," Yvonne said. "Yes. Twins."

Deniz made an exclamation, the Turkish version, it seemed, of *wow*. She translated for Captain Galip and he made the same exclamation. For her entire life as a mother, Yvonne had been getting credit for something over which she had no control. Twins ran in her family.

"What do they do, your childrens?" Deniz asked.

"My son is . . . he's about to get a job at a restaurant. He's a good cook, but he wants to manage restaurants. He's getting married next year."

"Next year is a giant year for him," Deniz said. Yvonne nodded. She didn't offer that every year for Matthew was a big one, full of accomplishments and celebrations. Peter had often listed them: National Merit Scholarship, early acceptance to Penn, second place in the regional lacrosse tournament, a pretty fiancée who had proposed to him, an offer—at age twenty-four—to be assistant manager of a restaurant that was booked two weeks in advance. If Matthew hadn't been her son, she would have thought life was too easy for him. Actually, she still believed that. Sometimes she feared he had received so many accolades, so much external affirmation, that he had been depleted and dulled on the inside. He rarely said anything that one wouldn't expect him to say.

"And your daughter?" Deniz asked. "Is she beautiful like

her mother?"

It was, Yvonne knew, the kind of compliment you received when you weren't in fact beautiful. "Thank you," she said, smiling. "We look similar, but she's much prettier."

Yvonne had spent a great deal of time assuring her daughter of her beauty. She had started when Aurelia was young, and people smiled briefly at her before their gazes landed on her twin brother, whose perpetually distracted eyes and slightly smug mouth lent him the air of someone who possessed a secret you wanted to know. The twins had the same nose, and on Matthew it appeared tough and authoritative while on Aurelia it looked indelicate, broken. Throughout their lives, Yvonne had made sure there were more pictures of Aurelia than Matthew on display on the fireplace mantel, in photo albums, and on holiday cards. Aurelia never commented on the disparity, but Yvonne was sure she noticed. Aurelia noticed everything.

"What does she do, your daughter?" Deniz asked.

"Well . . ." Yvonne started. She had long avoided questions about Aurelia—she and Peter both had. It had almost become a reflex. Galip interrupted then with a question, and, thankfully, Deniz turned her attention to him.

The first time Aurelia went to rehab, everyone asked, "What's your daughter up to?" because they didn't know. By her third stay in rehab, though, word had gotten around, and when people asked how Aurelia was, they were asking because they wanted to have the update for the next dinner party, the sort of parties that Yvonne and Peter had stopped going to. At a certain point Peter had found ways to avoid saying Aurelia's name.

When Deniz turned back to Yvonne, she had forgotten the topic of their conversation. "Your husband is on the beach?" She looked to shore, as though she might be able to spot him herself.

"I'm a widow," Yvonne said. She wasn't sure she had ever phrased it this way. Usually she just said her husband had passed away.

"What does that mean?"

"He's dead," Yvonne said, surprising herself. The words came too easily.

"I am sorry," Deniz said. She lifted her hand to her head, as though trying to imagine the pain, and fingered her head scarf. "I don't know I am still wearing this," she said, and removed it and folded it into a small rectangle. "I wear it when I cook. Some people on boat thinks it is for religion."

"Oh," said Yvonne. She'd assumed this too. "So you're not Muslim?"

"I am, but I pray in own way. I don't need to show my religion. You know how wife of Turkish president wears a head scarf?"

Yvonne shook her head.

"It's terrible. In this country Ataturk worked so hard for no religion in government, and now wife of Turkish president wears head scarf. Big problem. More iced tea?"

Deniz refilled her glass, and they sat in silence looking out at the water. "I think it is responsibility of spouse to watch what husband or wife does," Deniz said. "President should not let his wife wear a scarf. I learn long time ago to watch the Captain. Many year ago, I stay at home raising my children, and the Captain worked for Club Med. But I make him stop. I go one time on the boat and see many women, from Greece, from Danish, they all take off their shirts and sunbathe and eat without shirts and I tell the Captain, enough. I am going with you to keep eyes on you."

Yvonne said nothing. She knew this was how women spoke among each other, but she was out of practice. Since Peter's death, her friends had avoided any mention of their own marriages. At group lunches with five or six fellow teachers, all women, the word *husband* was not spoken. They conjured, by omission, an imaginary world without men.

"It is important for marriage, you know, to do this."

Yvonne nodded halfheartedly. Lately she had come to second-guess what she once thought important for a marriage.

Someone on a neighboring boat blasted an ABBA song for a moment, then turned it down. Yvonne and Deniz both stared in the direction of the music, as though daring it to assert itself again.

"This is a beautiful boat," Yvonne said.

"It's called a *gulet*. Is special to Turkey. More deck space for eating and sunbath."

"Does it have a name?"

"*Deniz II*," Deniz said. "It is named after me."

"So there was another *Deniz* before?"

"Yes, come, I show you." She stood and said something to Captain Galip, who had reappeared, and they all descended the steep stairs to the narrow passage in the galley, where framed black-and-white photos of the original *Deniz*, a smaller vessel, were on crowded display. Deniz and Galip pointed to pictures and announced proper names of people and companies, and it soon became apparent to Yvonne that they expected her to recognize their previous passengers. None of the names was familiar to Yvonne, but she nodded nonetheless to show approval of the caliber of *Deniz I*'s guests.

"I should go," Yvonne said to Deniz when they returned to the deck. She had already had two glasses of iced tea, and speaking English was becoming a burden to them both.

"If you please, come back and visit us," Deniz said as she walked Yvonne to the ladder.

"How long are you here?" Yvonne asked.

"Two days," Deniz said. "We do chartered boat trips each day, yes? Tomorrow we take German group to Rhodos, next day we go to Cleopatra's Island. Very pretty sand there. That day we have two Americans coming. Only two. Please, you are welcome."

"Okay," Yvonne said, "that would be nice. I'll join you the day after tomorrow—Friday—for Cleopatra's Island."

"We leave Knidos at ten, yes?"

"Okay." Yvonne was suddenly excited. She felt Deniz had something to teach her about being an older woman. Also, Yvonne had once been the kind of person who sought adventures, and she wanted to be that person again.

"Good," Deniz said. "I am very happy now."

"Me too," Yvonne said.

As Yvonne descended the ladder, the rungs sharp on her feet, she saw the laundry Deniz had been draping by the boat's railing when they had first started talking. Among the socks and shirts and towels hung a pair of Captain Galip's boxer shorts, which had once been white but were now the dull, grainy color of a cheap paperback. There was nothing sadder, Yvonne thought, than seeing an old man's underwear.

She dove off the bottom rung, and felt the stretch in her calves. The water was colder this time in, this far out. After swimming for a minute, she adjusted, and then took her time getting to shore.

Throughout much of her life Yvonne had made friends easily, and she attributed this to the fact that given any range of possibilities, she fell just to the right of middle: In terms of appearance, her features were neither beautiful nor harsh. Her dimples—she still had her dimples—tilted her to the attractive side of plain. She contributed to conversations without saying too much or too little, and she was smart without being intimidating. She walked into rooms never expecting anything but kindness, and in doing so, found she was greeted with open faces and quick intimacies.

In the past two years she had been different. She had welcomed nothing, had even assumed a pose in which she held one arm across her body as though to impede a potential embrace or attack. Her face too had changed; it appeared disapproving, even when Yvonne was not. She had worried for a time that the starchlike scent of death clung to her wherever she went, and she had taken to applying honeysuckle lotion to her arms, her neck.

But Deniz's kindness, her eagerness to share Yvonne's company, was reassuring to her. It felt like proof that this trip had been a good idea, and that Yvonne needed only to shed her cloak of mourning in order to be who she once was.

The water was murkier close to the beach, and Yvonne put her feet down to feel if it was shallow enough to stand. She almost scraped her knee on the rocks below. She staggered out of the water, trying to navigate the uneven surface between the weeds and, inexplicably, pieces of floating wood. Her body was cold as she emerged, but the warm air quickly blanketed her.

On the beach, a boy of about ten was laying something out on the sand. *Boys the world over had the same body*, she thought—narrow chests with protruding ribs and tiny paunches. He resembled Matthew at that age.

Yvonne walked past the boy, and saw he was organizing a collection of shells. He was setting them out with great care, the way a society hostess might arrange saucers and cups for a tea.

"What beautiful shells," she said, pausing in front of them. For a moment, she had forgotten she was in Turkey. The boy turned to her. He had wide pink lips and a straight nose and eyes that were moist and dark, as though they had recently teared.

Yvonne pointed to the shells and smiled, and he surprised her by not smiling back. She had had students like this boy, students who didn't immediately respond to her. It was the reluctant ones whose respect or attention she most pointedly sought.

She picked up a shell before noticing it was chipped on its side.

"Nice," she said, and smiled.

The boy said something and shook his head. He stood and pointed to the chip.

"Oh, I see," she said, holding it in her hand and pretending she hadn't already noticed it.

The boy said something else.

She was ashamed she hadn't learned any Turkish before arriving here. She and Peter used to study the basics before visiting any country—*hello, thank you, excuse me, where is the* . . . ?

"Pardon?" Yvonne said.

The boy held up his fingers. Two.

Of course—he was selling the shells. The elaborate layout on the beach was his shore-front display.

Yvonne tapped the sides of her hips, her hands grazing the edges of her swimsuit, as though to show she didn't have money on her.

The boy stared. *I am an idiot*, she thought. She felt the boy with his dark eyes must think so too.

She pointed to her towel on the beach, her small bag, and

started walking toward them. She realized she had left her belongings—her car keys, her money—on the beach while she had been on the boat. She sprinted toward her possessions as though hustling now could prevent any theft from having taken place in the past hour.

Everything was where she had left it. She turned to the boy and smiled at him, for she felt he was somehow responsible. He had not taken any of her possessions, nor had he let anyone else take them. She removed a five-lira note from her bag and handed it to him.

Now it was his turn to pat his hips—was he mocking her? He signaled to her to follow him back to the display of shells and began to speak Turkish again, as though if he continued speaking she might absorb his language during the very time he was talking to her.

Yvonne understood she was his first customer of the day, and because he had no change he wanted her to take more shells for her money. She pointed to one that more clearly resembled a sand dollar, and he nodded in approval. He knelt and, using a checkered cloth napkin, cleaned the sand from the shell before handing it to her.

"Thank you," she said. "Tea and sugar."

Yvonne returned to her beach towel, and as she sat down she again noticed the roughness of its texture. She closed her eyes to the sun, and her mind wandered to a fight she had had with Aurelia when Aurelia was a teenager. Aurelia had claimed that Yvonne loved her like any of her students, that she would have loved her if she had been bubbly or even dumb.

"Exactly," Yvonne said. "That's what being a parent is."

"But I want you to love me specifically for who I am," Aurelia said.

"Well, who are you, specifically?" Yvonne asked.

"See! You don't even know!"

Tears were forming in the corners of Yvonne's eyes. She wiped them away with her damp and sandy hands.

She heard laughter, and opened her eyes. The boy. He was standing in front of her, his shells wrapped in his towel and tossed over his shoulder. It appeared he had been walking past Yvonne and then stopped when something she had done amused him.

"What?" she said.

The boy pointed to her face. Then he dug down until he reached the darker patch of sand a few inches below the surface of the beach. He dipped his index finger and raised it and, with the wet sand, drew stripes on his face that started at his eyes and extended downward.

Yvonne understood. She took the edge of her towel and wiped away the sand on her cheeks. "All gone?" she said. "Better?"

The boy nodded. She was fine.

"Thank you," Yvonne said. The boy switched his grip on his towel and lifted the makeshift sack to the other shoulder. He waved to Yvonne and continued walking. *Don't leave*, she thought. She stared at his back, his small, narrow shoulders, and wished he would turn around. But he continued walking, and Yvonne was left alone.

She pressed a finger to the skin of her arms. Pink, like the inside of a shell. It had been a long time since she had exposed herself like this, and for so long. After taking a final dip in the ocean to cool her skin, she dried off carefully and completely, and made her way toward the parking lot.

A waiter at the restaurant gave her what seemed to be an unkind look as she walked past. Was that possible? *No,* she told herself. She drove back through Yakaköy, and this time stopped at the side of the road where an old woman sat on a low stool, hammering nuts on a small tree trunk. Yvonne rolled down the window and the woman stood and held out a large plastic bag of almonds. Their hands met as they made the exchange, and then they each nodded before Yvonne drove off. She bit into a large almond and could taste sun and dust. She ate another, and another, and vowed that each day she returned to Knidos—for she already knew she would spend the remaining days of her vacation in Knidos, her nights in Datça—she would buy almonds from a different woman standing by the side of the road.

Soon there was no one on the road, and the mountains around her seemed both taller and farther away. She felt loneliness seeping into her stomach, her chest, and she tried to stop it from spreading. It wouldn't be long before she saw Özlem and Deniz again, she told herself, and she was promptly rewarded with the small thrill that came with nascent friendship, with sharing life stories. Peter had been the one who got to tell the good stories and now, suddenly,

Yvonne longed for the opportunity to tell them herself. Or rather, she longed for the opportunity to see if she would tell them differently.

"Yvonne and I fell in love through the Italian postal service," Peter would say to anyone who asked. And, for the first fifteen years of their marriage, people asked all the time. *How did you meet?* They wanted to believe the secret to a happy marriage could be passed along like a recipe or remedy. Yvonne couldn't remember the last time she had told her version of how they met. Maybe this was what happened to any couple over the years: the anecdotes and family histories and jokes were divided up, much like household chores, and Peter had assumed the role of telling *their* story.

Yvonne was twenty-one and had been with someone else. Lawrence. Peter often left this name, *Lawrence*, out of the narrative. In fact, he left out everything to do with Lawrence, and just started the story midway through—after Yvonne and Lawrence had ended their relationship. If she had a chance to tell the story, Yvonne would start at the beginning.

Lawrence and Yvonne met at Stanford. Yvonne was there on a scholarship, the first in her family to go to college. He was there because all his relatives were Stanford alums, two of the buildings bearing his family's name. They met while working at the student radio station—he had a slot from four to six A.M., when he would play Latin dance music, and she read news from the AP wire at six. She started coming in to the station earlier and earlier, and he began waiting for her to finish her half hour of news so they could have breakfast together afterward.

A few times, they had gone away to his parents' second— or third—home in the wine country. They had exchanged kisses, but always stayed in separate rooms—that was part of the story. Details of those weekends at the country house were coming back to Yvonne now. All the newspapers: the family had six subscriptions to each Sunday paper, local and national, so no one would have to fight over copies. And the old stale Cokes in the kitchen cabinets. It was as though they had stocked up for a party ten years before. All the sodas were flat, their cans bearing a previous design incarnation that no longer existed.

Lawrence invited her to go on a trip to Europe together after they graduated. Europe! Her sisters had never been there, and spent months picking out outfits for her to wear along the Champs-Élysées, at the Prado, at canal-side dinners in Venice. She wrote postcards to her sisters from each city they visited. "Having a great time!" she'd scribble. That was all she said—anything else would reveal she was lying. She spent most of the days alone. Lawrence wanted to go off in the afternoons by himself—"It's good for us to have our space," he'd say. And strange things started happening. He came back to the hotel later and later, always with an excuse for his tardiness: he had been mugged, he had gotten lost, he had run into an old friend of his from Andover.

Yvonne would listen to his excuses, express her frustration, her worry, her concern, and then he'd say, "Darling, let me take you to dinner." And there they would drink red wine or white wine or champagne and eat three courses and talk and discuss and laugh and flirt—and then, before parting with her at her hotel door, he'd give her a firm but not unloving kiss.

Oh, she supposed she should have been thankful that he was a gentleman. Her sisters had told her she would owe him for the trip, that every night he would expect something from her. But the truth was Yvonne expected it too. She loved Lawrence for not fully wanting her, because it made her desperate and confused—all the things that in her youth she mistook for passion. And so one night in Florence, in their hotel by the Uffizi Palace, she washed herself with a pink shell-shaped soap he had bought her that day and dressed in the negligee her sisters had given her. With a hotel robe draped around her body and hotel slippers on her feet, she walked down the hall to his room. She wanted to believe she was playing the part, a woman unveiling herself to her intended for the first time.

She heard something behind the door, music and laughter, and took a step back to check that she had the right room. Room 19, his room. She knocked lightly and then more assertively—a strange panic was growing like a vine up her legs. Lawrence opened the door, his shirt off, and Yvonne forgot to adjust her plan. She let her robe open and drop to the floor behind her. And then she saw Lawrence was not alone. She should have known by Lawrence's face—he was not happy to see her. But behind him she saw a man pulling a robe around his naked body. The same hotel robe—the

Florentine flower stitched in gold on the pocket over the heart—that Yvonne had just let drop from her shoulders. A sound escaped her throat, passing through her lips before she could stop it. She ran back to her room, where she splashed her face with water and sat on the balcony for an hour, repeatedly counting the bridges of the Arno River, until the knocking at the door had finally stopped.

In the morning she saw him at breakfast.

"I'm sorry you found us," he said.

"You're sorry I found you, but not sorry about what you did."

"We could have had a great trip."

She did not tell him her parents expected that the European trip, for which his family was paying, meant they would return engaged. Yvonne and her sisters had shared the same room growing up, and when they had reunited in Albuquerque the previous Christmas, they'd spent the night in their old beds, in their old room, with their photos of prom nights and roller coaster rides, and invitations to high-school graduation parties still thumbtacked to the large, porous corkboard on their wall. It was there in that room, among these photos, that her sisters had planned her wedding for her—the ice with the mint leaf frozen within each cube, the dahlias, the million tiny silver stars that would be thrown instead of rice. She was surprised by how eagerly she greeted their conviction that she and Lawrence would marry.

She checked his face for signs of regret, and she saw it

there in his eyes and his cheeks, which had slackened into jowls overnight. He had plenty of regret, but all of it for himself. He regretted bringing her. Some other girl would have accepted the bargain, and gratefully.

"How I pity you," she said, and only a moment later, when he began to cry, did she realize this was true.

They spent the rest of the day in their separate rooms, writing notes to each other on hotel stationery. She would write three pages of a letter, fold it into quadrants, and slip it under the thick door to his room. Then she would pace around her bed, run the bathtub and fill it with bubbles (as though she could actually sit in a bathtub when waiting for his response) until his reply slid beneath her door. His letters were unfolded single sheets.

At the end of the day a decision had been reached. He would continue on the trip without her and she would remain in Florence until her scheduled flight home, in three weeks' time. She didn't want to return early because she didn't yet know what explanation she would give to her family. Nor did she have any interest in continuing on their planned itinerary, as he suggested. He could see Switzerland and its mountains and Austria and its white horses without her.

The next morning when he came to her door to say goodbye he looked like a person who had been relieved of a lie. Staring at him, Yvonne thought of an amateur painting she had once seen in which the seated figure cast no shadow, bore no relationship to the ground beneath him.

"I'll write to you," he said.

"I'm not going to keep staying here," she said, gesturing to the rug of the hotel room behind her, as though the small rug was where she spent her time.

"Then I'll write to you care of *poste restante*."

"Okay," she said, as though she knew what this meant.

"It's a box they keep at every main post office, anywhere you go. Since you don't know where you're staying . . ."

"Okay," she said again.

They parted without touching. He left her a purple purse with a gold clasp, a farewell present. She was not surprised when, later, she opened it and found money inside. Enough to last her three weeks in Florence.

She informed the front desk she would be staying another night and set out to find other, less expensive, accommodations. The next day, she found a flat above a bakery, shared by two women her age. They were art restoration students, German and Italian, serious but warm. She paid for a month's stay in advance.

There remained the question of what to do with herself. For the first few days, she planned small trips—to Bologna, where she bought green peppers at the outdoor market, to Arezzo, where she walked up the steep hills and ate a picnic of salami and focaccia in a garden overlooking the town's clock towers, none of which chimed the hour at the same time. But after three days of trips, she felt tired and stayed in the apartment, the smell of flour wafting up from the bakery below.

On the fifth day she accepted her roommates' invitation

to visit them at school to see their work. She arrived in the morning and observed them in the large windowless room, seated before various canvases. It was not engaging work to watch; after two hours, she could detect little progress. But she loved the room with all the women—the students were primarily female—restoring paintings that had been damaged by dampness or smoke or transport. *This is what women do*, she thought vaguely, *we restore things, we make them right.*

After leaving the school in the late afternoon, she walked to the main post office to see if Lawrence had written.

"*Poste restante*," Yvonne said to the woman behind the counter. The woman brought out a large tin box and instructed Yvonne to stand to the side and search through it while the next customer was helped.

The box was cold to the touch, its surface like a watering can, and not as well organized as Yvonne would have expected. Inside were at least a hundred envelopes and postcards, many folded or torn at their corners, from all parts of the world. She sorted through postcards from Tasmania and Newfoundland, letters postmarked from Amsterdam and Stockholm, Atlanta and Cape Town, but found nothing from Lawrence addressed to her. It had been almost a week and she should have heard from him by now. Even if it was another apology.

When she reached the back of the box she turned over the final postcard, hoping it was for her. It was addressed to a woman named Frederica, and was written in English. The handwriting, tilted far to the right, was the most unusual

Yvonne had ever seen. She read the note:

> *Dear Frederica,*
>
> *Only two weeks until I see you. You don't know how anxious I am. After you left, teaching, once a pleasure, as you know, became a burden. The students are good. "Where is Ms. Frederica?" they said. They tease me about being in love, and what can I say? I can't lie to them.*
>
> *Love, Peter*

Yvonne turned the card over. It was a picture of the library at Alexandria, Egypt.

Yvonne left the post office, the smear of ink and the damp metallic smell of the box still on her hands. She walked past the tourists following guides carrying brightly-colored parasols, past the bored salesgirls standing by store windows.

The next afternoon Yvonne returned to the post office. Another postcard written in the slanted handwriting had arrived from Peter.

> *Dear Frederica,*
>
> *I received your letter just today and I'm so confused. What do you mean that I'm a distant fixture in your life? It has only been a month. You don't know the state you've left me in. I will stay awake until I see you. Please, if you misspoke or were just in a strange mood when you wrote, please write again as soon as possible.*

My heart can't take this wait, these words.
    Love, Peter

Yvonne turned the postcard around—another photo of the library at Alexandria, this one taken from within. Her fingers ran through the rest of the mail in the box. She was less interested in seeing whether Lawrence had written than she was to see whether Frederica had retrieved Peter's last correspondence. It was still there. Yvonne read it twice, before placing it in the front of the box, where it would surely be discovered if someone was looking for it.

That week she could think of nothing but the post office. Sunday, when it was closed, seemed interminable. She walked around Florence, staring at the watermark lines on the buildings that showed how high the river had risen during the flood of 1333.

On Monday, she forced herself to take a bus to Fiesole before going to the post office. If she checked the mail first thing in the morning, the rest of the day would be too long. She happened upon a string quartet playing inside a small church, and closed her eyes and tried to listen. When the concert was over, she caught the first bus back to Florence. A scooter almost hit her as she raced to the doors of the post office.

She quickly flipped through the more recent arrivals, in search of any mail from Egypt. The box was emptier today and she noted that Paolo had finally retrieved the letters that awaited him from Spain, that Ann and Erica had picked up the birthday wishes sent from America. Toward the middle of the box was a new postcard from Peter, the writing more slanted, as though it was on the precipice of tumbling off the edge.

> *Dear Frederica,*
>
> *I'll be in Florence next Tuesday. I have no other way to reach you so I hope you receive this in time. I'll wait for you from noon on in front of the Grotta del Buontalenti in the Boboli Gardens. I saw a picture of it in the library here. I hope that you'll come to meet me— even if it is to say good-bye.*
>
> *Love, Peter*

Tomorrow Peter would be waiting at the Grotta del Buontalenti. Yvonne's heart raced. She knew she would go watch him from afar, and she too would wait to see if Frederica showed up.

Yvonne awoke Tuesday morning to the sound of pigeons fighting outside her window. She planned out her day carefully—allowing an hour to shower and choose her clothes, an hour for breakfast. She could easily dress and eat in the span of fifteen minutes, but that would leave too much time for waiting.

At half past eleven she walked to the Boboli Gardens. She knew from her dictionary that *grotta* meant *cave*, but she had never seen or heard of the Grotta del Buontalenti before and had difficulty finding it. At noon she began to panic. She asked everyone she could if they knew where it was. But she was surrounded only by tourists carrying the same guidebook, which failed to show the Grotta on its map. She was sweating as she walked quickly from east to west of the gardens, then north to south. Then she zigzagged, until finally, near the edge of the gardens, close to the entrance, she saw a sign for the Grotta del Buontalenti. She was so stunned she paused in front of the arrow, as though the direction itself was all she'd been seeking.

Her steps quickened as she approached the cave. No one was in sight, and for a moment she feared she had missed Peter. But even more, she feared that she had missed them both, that Frederica had visited the *poste restante* box that morning, and had come here to be reunited. She had missed it all.

Yvonne walked closer to the Grotta, access to which was prohibited by a railing. She read on a sign that the cave was a man-made creation, designed by Buontalenti in the sixteenth century. It consisted of four chambers, only the first of which was immediately visible. Yvonne looked up. From the muddy walls of the cave, sculptures of slaves were fighting to emerge. Behind the first chamber of the cave was another, in the center of which stood a sculpture of a man and woman, their bodies entwined. Lovers.

She was thinking of how she could come back at night and go inside, travel deeper into the Grotta, to the other chambers, when she felt a hand on her shoulder. She jumped. A guard, she imagined, was reading her trespassing thoughts.

But no, it was a young man of twenty-four or twenty-five, only a few years older than she. He was tall, his hair blond and his skin tan, with a spray of freckles the color of sand gathered around his squinted green eyes.

"Excuse me," the man said in English. "I thought . . ."

"You thought I was someone else," Yvonne said.

The man nodded, and as he did so he stared at Yvonne and she saw something peculiar wash over his face. Instead of being disappointed, he looked relieved. His eyes remained squinting—she understood this was their permanent state, which lent him the air of constantly observing something through a microscope—but his hand, still on her shoulder, relaxed.

"Sorry," he said, and removed it from her body.

"It's okay," she said.

"I'm Peter," he said.

She nodded. She knew this.

"And you are?" he asked.

"Yvonne," she said. "From New Mexico."

He turned then and looked at the Grotta del Buontalenti. "I wish I could step over and go to the second room."

"I was planning on coming back at night," confessed Yvonne.

"I'll join you," he said, surprising them both. "I'm sorry if that was forward. I've just traveled from Egypt and I'm a bit . . . discombobulated."

Yvonne bit her lip. She was afraid of saying something too knowing. She made note of the fact that he had not mentioned Alexandria. She would have to make sure not to bring it up herself. They sat down on a bench placed before the Grotta.

"What were you doing there?" she asked. "In Egypt?"

"Teaching English," he said, and smiled with one side of his face. "What have you been doing in Florence?"

"Learning Italian."

They spoke easily, without pause, and she admired him for not looking around, for not telling her he was waiting to meet someone there, at this very spot. If he was discouraged, he didn't show any sign.

When three hours, maybe more, had passed, he stood and took her hands, bringing her to her feet. "What do we do now?" he said, though he had brought her so close their lips were almost touching.

When Yvonne arrived at the main road that would take her to Datça, she pushed down on the accelerator, relieved to be free of turns and hills. But everyone around her was driving well below the speed limit, as though they were lost and looking. Soon she was driving faster than the other cars, which had started pulling off onto the shoulder of the road to let her pass. They honked their horns at her and flashed their lights as though saluting her speed. She felt bold, strong. Colors and shapes splashed against her windshield.

She rolled down the window to feel the air rushing on her

skin, and immediately smelled something bitter and burnt. Tar.

Yvonne slowed the car enough to see tar had recently been poured on the road. Only now did she remember the tar trucks she had trailed that morning, the ones that had slowed traffic. She pulled to the side and hesitated before stepping out. When she did, she was more shocked than she expected to be. The white car was now a brown so deep it was almost black, purplish in the sun. She put her finger to the hood. The tar was thick, the top layer still malleable, while the bottom layers appeared to have already dried.

Now her mind was full again, this time with practical questions: *How would she remove the tar? How much would it cost? How would she get the tar off her finger? How could she be such an idiot?*

Yvonne drove back to the house slowly, which was unnecessary when she thought about it; the damage was done. But she didn't want to face the blinks of headlights or the honks of horns now that she knew what they were really saying: *Lady, are you insane?*

She pulled the car up to the front of the house. Leaving the motor running, she stepped out to the garage. She tried to lift the garage door by its silver handle. It wouldn't budge. She tried inserting each of the keys on her ring into the lock. Nothing fit. She would have to park the ruined car on the street until she figured out what to do.

The maid and her family had left—a relief. She didn't

want the woman to see the car and attempt to clean it. Yvonne wandered through the rooms—the clean floors had been mopped, the clean dishes washed. Upstairs, new sheets had been put on the master bed; the pillowcases, propped against the headboard, were blue with yellow birds. The maid had no reason to think Yvonne wouldn't sleep in this room. The sheets on the twin bed where she had slept had not been changed.

Yvonne washed her hands, and then opened the laptop Matthew and Callie had given her. Since arriving in Turkey she had resisted checking her e-mail; she was trying to avoid any news from Aurelia. At any given time Aurelia was bound to have been insulted on the street or fired from a job, or be suffering from an incurable earache, migraine, eye inflammation, or food poisoning.

The wireless signal was strong—Yvonne now remembered "Internet" had been listed as one of the features of the rental—and she did a search for *tar* and *car*. A *children's rhyme*, she thought. *A child's mistake.* There were a number of solutions, the first involving applying peanut butter to the car and waiting twenty-four hours to remove it. If that didn't work, WD-40 was recommended, though with it came the risk of damaging the paint.

It was too far to walk to the supermarket, so Yvonne reluctantly drove. Fearful of making eye contact with anyone, she kept her gaze on the road in front of her. *Ridiculous*, she told herself. *No one here knows who I am. I am anonymous.* But then she corrected herself: no one is anonymous when they're driving a car coated in tar.

She sank lower in the driver's seat. She was reminded of Matthew before the age of six, when Yvonne and Peter would find him under coffee tables and picnic benches, picking his nose or pulling down his underwear. "God can't see me here," he would say. That was shortly before they stopped going to church.

At the supermarket, Yvonne searched for peanut butter but didn't find any. No one in Turkey ate peanut butter, it appeared. She looked for WD-40, and when she couldn't find it she selected what looked to be its closest equivalent, something called Power Creme. Buckets and rags were easy to locate, as were plain paper towels. One multipack came, inexplicably, with a small stuffed white elephant. She settled on this package even though it contained twelve rolls, more than she would ever need; she could give the elephant to the boy in Knidos.

After parking in front of the house, she reassessed the damage she had done. Now that she had a potential plan for correcting her mistake, she could face the car without averting her eyes. It looked as though it had been dipped into a vat of chocolate. She lifted her plastic bags from the passenger seat, and the weight of her cleaning supplies stretched the handles uncomfortably over the tender skin of her palms.

Yvonne almost never drank alone, but now as she entered the Datça house, she spotted the wine bottle on the kitchen counter and searched for a wine opener. There were three in a utensils drawer. The cork released itself from the bottle with the sound of a theatrical kiss.

The sound of a liberated cork had disturbed Yvonne ever since the night she and Peter had returned from driving Aurelia to the first of many rehab centers. (As Aurelia's dependency became more dire, they began taking her by plane to centers in Minnesota, then Arizona—as though the greater the distance they traveled, the more likely her recovery would be.) As soon as they walked in the door after the drive, Peter walked straight to the kitchen and opened a bottle of wine.

"What are you doing?" she asked.

Peter took a sip before responding. "I need a drink," he said.

"I don't know if we should be doing this," said Yvonne.

"She's the one with the problem. You and I, we've never had anything."

"But out of respect . . ."

"Out of respect!" Peter stammered. For a moment his face looked as if it might break into laughter, before it transformed itself into an expression of anguish. "If she had any respect for this family, she wouldn't have brought us to this point. Respect! She doesn't care about anything!"

"Don't yell at me," Yvonne said.

"I'm sorry," Peter said. "I'm sorry."

"It's not that she doesn't care about anything," Yvonne said. "She cares about everything. Any comment that's made to her, she holds onto it like it's been knitted to her skin.

She's just trying to dull the pain of feeling everything."

"Well, at least she's *passionate* about something," Peter said. He hissed the word.

"What's that supposed to mean?"

"You're the one who said you didn't care if the kids played sports or piano or . . . planted gardens, as long as they were passionate."

"I still believe that," Yvonne said.

"Well, now look what your daughter's passionate about."

"Are you saying the self-medicating is my fault? That her addiction is . . . please tell me what you're saying."

They'd had versions of this conversation before, and this time Peter wasn't listening. "Poor Matthew," he said.

"Poor Matthew? Poor Aurelia," Yvonne said. "It isn't easy for her to be his sister. It would be hard for anyone."

She wanted to add, *Though I know it's easy for you to be his father*, but she didn't. This wasn't the time for that, though she resented the pride Peter took in Matthew, the way he put his arm around him after a lacrosse game as they walked to the car, as if to say to everyone, *That's right. This star is mine.* The way Peter spoke too loudly when in his presence, so that everyone around them—at a street fair, a pool, an airport—would know they were together, a unit. But when Peter was with Aurelia, his voice often dropped to a whisper. "What?" Aurelia would yell. She knew. She always knew. "I can't hear you."

Matthew was never unkind to Aurelia, which in some ways, Yvonne believed, further infuriated his sister. Aurelia wanted him to be unfair to her so she could tell on him. She wanted him to exclude her from his parties, his lunch table, so she could hate him. But he did none of these things. As their mother, Yvonne was alone in seeing the truth: that in his own way, Matthew was terrified of his sister. He treated her like she was already gone. He spoke of her with deference and empathy, as one speaks of the dead.

Yvonne stood at the kitchen counter in the rented house in Datça, swallowing large gulps of Mr. Çelik's wine. It was viscous, simultaneously sour and sweet, like cherry juice. Her thighs were suddenly sore, trembling. Her body was tired from the swim, the sun, the drive; her physical fatigue yet another reminder that she was no longer young. She filled her glass again.

The doorbell rang. A neighbor, Yvonne thought, coming to complain about the eyesore parked outside. Her head was light and she walked with small steps to the door. Özlem. Yvonne was so relieved to see Özlem that she fell into her arms.

"What happened?" Özlem said. "Tell me." There was urgency in her voice, as though Yvonne had just been robbed and there was still a chance of catching the thief.

Yvonne couldn't speak. When she released herself from the embrace, she saw Özlem's dress was damp on the shoulder where Yvonne had rested her cheek. She lifted her fingers to her own face, and only then did she know she had been crying.

"Did you see the car outside?"

Özlem shook her head. "Did you have an accident?"

Yvonne shook her head too. "I just . . . I'm sorry."

Özlem went to the window and looked outside. "I see. Should we clean the car?"

Yvonne was grateful she was taking the initiative, that she was using the word *we*. She followed Özlem into the kitchen. She had to remind herself that this was not Özlem's kitchen, but that of her husband's lover. Özlem removed a roll of paper towels, frowned, and then pursed her lips as though looking for something else.

"I'll bring this out," Yvonne said, reaching for the Power Creme. Özlem raised her eyebrows into a quizzical expression.

"From the Internet," Yvonne explained. "They recommended this."

The two women walked outside together in silence. There was only the slapping of Özlem's sandals on the steps.

"It's okay. We'll fix this," said Özlem.

Yvonne opened the Power Creme. The scent was strong and stung her eyes.

Özlem was wearing a brown-and-white checkered shift dress that reached mid-thigh. When she lifted her arms up, the dress followed, just barely covering the edge of her underwear. And yet she set to work right away, her thin arms working the towels over the car. She let out a few small and primal grunts, the kind a tennis player might make when returning a serve.

Yvonne scrubbed one side of the car and Özlem the other. The Power Creme appeared to be working. Each time they were finished with a paper towel, they tossed the loose sticky ball of it into a pile on the side of the road. It was Özlem who thought to go inside and get garbage bags. Yvonne watched her as she returned down the steps. She didn't sprint carelessly the way Yvonne would have done at her age, but instead walked almost at a diagonal down the stairs, with poise, as though she were competing in the swimsuit portion of a beauty contest. They went back to scrubbing the car.

"I'm feeling this in my arms," Yvonne said. "What about you?"

"I like being sore," said Özlem. "It makes me feel like I've done something."

Yvonne wondered how Özlem passed her days. "I can't thank you enough for helping me," she said. "You really didn't need to."

"It's not a problem," said Özlem, stopping to wipe her brow with the back of her forearm.

"Almost done," Yvonne said as they carried the trash down the road to the large garbage bins. A striped cat was perched on the edge of one, peering inside. Together they stood, assessing their work from afar.

"Perfect," Özlem said.

Yvonne laughed. It was far from perfect.

"Should we celebrate?" Özlem said.

"What, finishing the car?"

"No, life!" Özlem said this with such strained enthusiasm that it was clear she too was going through a difficult time.

Inside the house, Yvonne carried a glass of wine out to Özlem. She was sitting on the couch, and Yvonne felt ashamed that she had not yet moved the naked picture of Ali's lover from underneath.

"I brought you something," Özlem said as she rummaged through her bag.

"Thank you."

"You don't know what it is yet." Özlem handed a book to Yvonne. "It's for writing down everything you want to remember. The people from Dove gave me a few. I don't want you to think I'm pretending I bought it."

"Thank you," Yvonne said, holding it in her hands. The book had a mirror on its cover. "It's still a lovely thought, whether you bought it or not."

They sat in silence for a moment.

"Can I ask you something?" said Yvonne.

"Yes."

"About the car . . . I can't expect you to keep secrets from your husband, but would you consider not telling him?"

Özlem laughed. Someone must have told her she had a nice laugh because she seemed to know it. Her laugh lasted for a few seconds longer than it needed to.

"My husband doesn't own the car. I think maybe he just asked someone he knew who rents cars. Why would I tell him? Besides, I have better secrets to keep from him."

"What do you mean?" Yvonne said.

Özlem was making it clear she was going to take her time with this one. Even the air between them seemed to be dented, waiting to be straightened again.

At last Özlem spoke. "I found out today. I'm pregnant."

Yvonne searched Özlem's face for a sign of how she felt about this. Yvonne wasn't sure how she felt about this. "Congratulations!" she said.

Özlem nodded.

"I met a man in Istanbul. And it could belong to him. I do not know."

Yvonne tried not to let her mouth drop. "Does Ali know about the man in Istanbul?"

"No," said Özlem, and then said it again. She pushed the glass of wine away from her. "I don't know what I'm going to do. What do you think?"

"I think you have to tell the truth," said Yvonne. "I think sooner or later you have to."

"But maybe he won't find out it's not his."

"Well, would you tell him it's his when it's not?" Yvonne said.

"If I tell him the truth, Ali will leave me," Özlem said, as though it had just occurred to her.

"Didn't you already leave him?" Yvonne said, suddenly lost. She was easily exhausted by the romantic dramas of the young.

"You probably never kept secrets from your husband," said Özlem.

"That's not true," Yvonne said, and paused.

Özlem looked at her expectantly. "Tell me."

This was Yvonne's chance to tell a story to someone who hadn't known Peter. She thought of what example to give, of where to start. There was a period when they began hiding things from each other, when the twins were sixteen.

"You really want to hear about my marriage right now?"

Özlem nodded convincingly.

"It was maybe eight years ago," Yvonne said before she knew which story she was going to tell. "I was taking my students to D.C. on a field trip. An educational trip to Washington, D.C. Where the White House is?"

Özlem closed her eyes as though to show she knew this, of course she did, and that she would let the offense pass if Yvonne continued quickly.

"There are a lot of museums there and I was taking my advanced students—I teach history. There was another teacher at our high school at the time who was teaching a similar class, and he was co-chaperoning the trip, making sure the boys didn't get into trouble. His name was Joseph. A couple times, Peter suggested Joseph had a crush on me. I always brushed it off, told him he was crazy, but mostly because I knew he was right. I could feel Joseph stare at me for too long, and once, before we were supposed to meet for coffee to discuss the syllabus, I saw him combing his hair in front of the side mirror of his car."

"Did you like him?" Özlem said.

"He was charming. He was from New Zealand and had a lovely accent. He made me feel that whatever I said was very,

very important."

"And you were on a trip together?"

"Well, it was us and twenty-two students," said Yvonne. "But that night, at four in the morning, the phone rang in my hotel. At first I thought it was an emergency, that one of the students was in trouble. But when I picked up the phone there was no one there. Just a click as the caller hung up. I couldn't go back to sleep after that."

"Was it Joseph?"

Yvonne shook her head. "I waited for the phone to ring again and it didn't. When I got back home on Sunday evening, I mentioned to Peter over dinner that a phone call in the middle of the night had kept me from going back to sleep. Peter suggested it might have been one of the students playing a joke. But something about the way he said it, the way he was so quick to give a reason, made me think things I didn't want to think."

Yvonne took a long sip of her wine.

"A few weeks later the phone bill arrived, and in spite of myself, I checked the long-distance calls that had been made the weekend I was in Washington. I was hoping I wouldn't see it, but there it was. Peter had made a four A.M. phone call to my hotel, and hung up on me, his wife."

"He wanted to check that you were in your room?" said Özlem.

"He wanted to make sure I wasn't with Joseph."

"And you never told him you know it was him."

"No. I knew it would humiliate him somehow, that I knew he had been jealous enough to do such a thing."

"Had you ever been unfaithful to him? Why was he suspectful?"

"No, never," Yvonne said. She considered telling Özlem that, because of the way they had met, through the *poste restante*, Peter was occasionally concerned she would fall sneakily, whimsically in love with someone else.

She opted for a more basic explanation. "Our daughter was going through a difficult period, and she was lying to us a lot, and Peter started feeling that anyone could lie to him. I know it doesn't make sense, but distrust . . . it's a viral thing."

"It makes sense," Özlem said. "It does."

Yvonne shrugged, as though to say, *All that can be said has been said.* "What are you going to do?" she asked, determined to return the conversation to Özlem.

"I don't know yet," Özlem said.

Yvonne nodded, and then finished her glass of wine. "I'll stop by tomorrow," Özlem promised, and left.

They had exchanged confidences—Özlem's large, Yvonne's small—within the course of a short time, and now they both seemed ready to escape the room in which the inequality of these confessions had been voiced.

Yvonne heated a frozen pizza for dinner. While she was waiting for the pizza's crust to brown, she drank Özlem's glass of wine. It was not good, but she enjoyed it immensely. What a silly, insignificant story she had shared. She was free to tell whatever story she wanted to a new and impartial listener, and this is what she had chosen?

She moved outside to the patio to eat and began to read the first page of her novel. It was a thin book she had read many years before, about a woman's love affair with an older man when she was a teenager.

One day, I was already old . . .

Yvonne read the line three times. She felt far beyond her own years. Age had not crept up on her gradually, but rather had dropped down on her like a net. Not immediately after Peter's death, as she might have expected. No, in the weeks afterward she had purpose. There was the service, the lawyers, the insurance people offering her pointless advice: "I know it's too late now, but next time you get car insurance, don't skimp on uninsured motorist coverage."

The idea of opening mail was hard enough. The condolence cards with their sad flowers and gray clouds suggesting—what? Heaven? A rainstorm? And banal words. "Thinking of you at this time." "With sympathy." With sympathy! They should have said, "With fear." Or, "With relief." Yvonne knew that everyone who wrote to her was thankful that a member of their own families, their spouses, had not been killed. Wasn't everyone a gambler, a statistician? The fact that Peter had been killed decreased the chances that they would lose their husbands, their wives, their children.

Yvonne had made a point of not crying during the service. She had cried all morning before it began and cried when everyone had gone home, but she would not cry while reading the Auden poem Peter had loved and that now seemed too appropriate; she would not cry when others teared up upon seeing her. Her tears were private—for him alone, not for show.

Adjectives abounded the day of the service, adjectives about Peter's life: wonderful father, loving husband, devoted teacher. And later about Yvonne. How brave! they said. How strong! So amazing! What a fun-loving but devoted couple they had been, how many students they had helped educate and nurture. The students at the funeral looked down at their own palms whenever they were mentioned, as though trying to weigh the import of their teacher's death on their own lives.

Yvonne detested the vapidity of adjectives, their prevalence, their interchangeability. How wonderful and strong their love had been! How fun and amazing their marriage had been. What a devoted father, loving teacher, wonderful husband he had been. What a devoted husband, loving father, wonderful teacher. It meant less every time someone pressed their hands into hers and looked at her meaningfully. *Please stop*, she had wanted to say to them all. *Please stop talking. None of this is working.*

After the service, after everyone had left, she caught her reflection in a bathroom mirror, and was astounded at how young she looked. She looked eighteen. Her face was flush and tight, her eyes shone without filter. Three months later, after she had dealt with the lawyers and written thank-you notes for the flowers, it was as though she was walking into the water and suddenly the ocean floor fell from her feet: she looked in the mirror and she was old, old, old.

Yvonne made her way up the red-railed spiral staircase. The air, usually cool by evening, was still hot. She opened the window in the bedroom and it promptly shut itself again.

Upstairs, she recalled, was a sliding door to the balcony. She could open that window without it slamming shut. She climbed the stairs to the top floor and saw the contraption was still there, laid out on the bed. But the maid seemed to have adjusted it; now it looked like the figure at the end of a game of hangman. Yvonne picked it up—it was heavier than she expected—and folded it into an unwieldy shape, placing it under the bed. It was still conspicuous. A colorfully painted trunk, depicting what looked like a fox hunt, sat at the foot of the bed. Yvonne opened it tentatively, and was relieved to see only blankets and sheets. She placed the contraption inside and closed the lid.

She slid open the door to the balcony. The night air was warm. Yvonne paused as she looked out on the red rooftops below, pink in the moonlight. Datça was prettier now, all its blemishes hidden in the blue night.

Downstairs, she washed her face, and while standing at the sink, the wine hit her all at once. She used the walls for balance as she made her way to the twin bed. When she landed on the mattress, she sighed, very happy to be free of the obligations of standing.

Her eyes were closed and her mind was unstable. She gripped the side of the mattress to keep herself steady. *I should drink water*, she told herself, but she knew if she got up she might fall. So she held onto the bed and her thoughts spun.

Aurelia had been ten or eleven when one night, at a neighbor's wedding, she consumed two pieces of cake and, high on sugar, wanted to dance. Yvonne had taken her out to the makeshift dance floor, and they held hands. Without speaking, Aurelia initiated their movements. They each lifted one arm overhead until they were facing away from each other, their fingers straining to keep hold of the other's hand, before turning toward each other again. Right arm up, left arm up. Around and around the two of them spun, and each time their eyes met Yvonne saw that what everyone said was true: Aurelia's eyes did indeed resemble her own— they were cloudy and dense, the color of a substance that, heavier than everything else, had settled to the bottom of a glass. Right arm, left arm. Yvonne had felt light from the spinning, from the wonder of genetics—of birth!—and yet, at the same time, she experienced a sinking responsibility for having brought this girl into the world. In the course of one dance, she had witnessed all Aurelia's vulnerability and kindness, and the enormity of her daughter's emotions— the fragility of her joy and the intensity of her pain—had hit Yvonne with such force that finally she had to stop the twirling and say, as cheerfully as she could, "Okay. That's enough."

In the morning Yvonne awoke with her face tucked into her elbow. The heavy wine had now coursed through her blood and soured. Her skin smelled like old armor.

She walked downstairs, gripping the railing tightly. Her balance was uneven, her hands clammy. The marble was cool to her feet. As she approached the first floor, the strength of the sun was frightening. On the dining room table lay the Dove book Özlem had brought her. The mirror on its cover was meant to announce the beauty of anyone who looked into it. Yvonne caught her reflection and winced.

She made her way into the kitchen, where she scooped grounds into the cone filter of the coffeemaker, added water, and stood watching as it made its waking noises. The machine was in the corner of the kitchen, near the sink, and Yvonne could smell a strong odor. Garbage? She looked— almost nothing in the trash can. She checked the sink itself. A piece of sausage that had come off her pizza when she'd rinsed her plate, but that was all.

She removed a coffee mug from the cabinet, saw that it said TURKEY IS FOR LOVERS, put it back, and took out a smaller mug that was bare save for a turquoise rim. She walked to the dining room table, all the while feeling as if someone was watching her. She turned and something caught her eye. In the top corner of the kitchen, above the coffeemaker, there was something brown, feathered, oval. An owl.

Yvonne almost gagged. The smell—that meaty, musty odor—must have come from the bird. Was it dead? No, it was asleep. A brown owl, its feathers pulled around its torso like a cloak. She could call Mr. Çelik but she felt funny about him now, knowing what she knew. If she opened the window would the owl leave? Should she chase him out with a broom? How did it get in? She recalled opening the sliding door of the room on the top floor the night before.

She rose slowly, all the while keeping her eye on the owl, which appeared to be sleeping. She walked backward to the staircase and then quickly went upstairs, where she changed into her yellow swimsuit, pulled a sundress over her head, and gathered what she would need for the day. She would leave the house to the owl and hope it would depart on its own. When she returned cautiously downstairs, the owl was still small, sleeping. She left the front door propped open, enough so the owl could see the sky and find its way out, and locked the gate at the base of the stairs.

She had almost forgotten about the car, about the tar and the Power Creme. From the gate the car looked good, back to normal. But as she approached the Renault, she saw that in patches, the paint had been ruined. Here and there, the car now had the pale yellow and thin texture of a daisy petal held up to the light.

She thought of the cost. She didn't have the vaguest idea of how much it would be to repair the damage. Maybe, she decided, she could return the car in the evening, when its flaws were less likely to show.

She carefully draped the beach towel over the hot driver's seat and drove into town. She parked near a small corner store, where she bought two large wreaths of bread from behind an outdoor display counter, a carton of orange juice, and the largest bottle of water she could find.

She drove with the bottle of water sweating between her thighs and with both hands on the wheel as she navigated the road to Knidos, which seemed both longer and curvier today. She noticed every bump beneath her. The hills looked as though they had been scorched since the day before.

When she came to Yakaköy she spotted a hotel on her right, a colorful chateau on a hill, with sun umbrellas that promised a pool. She was tempted to check in there for the rest of the week. She could leave behind the owl and the sex swing, the book about anal sex, the twin bed. But then there was Özlem. And the deposit. She couldn't abandon it. It was unlike her to entertain such a frivolous thought.

As she passed through the town she watched the old women sitting along the road, in front of their small wooden tables, hammering and pounding the nuts. Yvonne recalled her promise to buy something from a different vendor each day, but she had already forgotten what yesterday's woman looked like.

She slowed the car and bought a bag of almonds from a woman she couldn't be sure wasn't the same one she had bought from before, and, as though to compensate for her own confusion, for the possibility of breaking her own oath to herself, she stopped the car a few hundred feet down the road and bought a jar of honey from another woman. Each transaction took place over the transom of the driver's door window. The women seemed grateful, but she felt silly. What was she going to do at the beach with a jar of honey?

There was no shade in the Knidos parking lot, and the heat enveloped her like a flannel coat. She passed the restaurant, and with small footsteps—even walking was exhausting—made her way to the beach. She sat on the sand with her water and bread and looked for the boy, for his shells. He was nowhere in sight, and Yvonne was surprised by her own disappointment.

She broke off small pieces of bread and ate them slowly. As the day accosted her, she could smell stale wine leaving her body. Yvonne sipped from her water bottle until it was empty and grunted as she lifted herself to her feet and walked toward the sea. She dipped her toes in the small wave that fizzled on the shore. The chill, the warmth. She waded in.

When the water was waist-high, she dove in and swam every stroke she knew. She kicked out, out, out with no destination in mind. Ahead and to her left, she saw something white. She turned. A kickboard floating, with no one in sight. It rose and fell with the water, and she began to swim toward it. The next time she looked up she saw a boy hoisting himself onto the kickboard. It was her boy. She waved her arms as though signaling to an airplane above.

The boy looked in her direction, lifted a hand, and pointed to the shore. Yvonne made it back there first, and stood on the beach, waiting for him. She could see he was balancing the shells he had found on the front of the kickboard. He kicked from behind, keeping the board steady. The shells rattled but none fell. When the water became shallow, he slid off the board carefully and carried it like a tray. All of it—the kicking, the way he made his way out of the water—was so effortless and assured. He walked toward Yvonne, smiling his big white smile, his eyes bright. They had no method of greeting but this—wide smiles, nods. He began to lay the shells out before her, in neat rows.

"Lovely," she said, examining the shiniest one. "Nice to see you," she added, unable to contain herself. She was so happy to be with him.

"Nice to see you," he said, imitating her.

They were both silent for a moment, looking at the shells between them.

"Oh, I brought you something," she said, and offered him the elephant that had come with the paper towels. She had packed it in her bag. He looked at it, unimpressed, and as he held it in his hand she saw what a ridiculous offering it was. A baby's toy. She took it back from him and extended the bag of almonds, which seemed to please him.

To break the quiet, she told him about the owl in her house. She didn't mind that he probably couldn't understand any of what she was saying; he was an attentive listener. It was possible, she thought, that he liked the sound of her voice. She had a good speaking voice—Peter called it soothing—and a small part of why she had become a teacher had to do with the way others responded when she spoke. Why wouldn't her voice sound just as good to someone who couldn't understand what she was saying? It might sound better.

The boy ate her almonds while she spoke. He ate them one at a time, carefully, unselfishly, not like a boy at all.

"Can I treat you to lunch?" Yvonne offered. "I'm starving," she said. Now that the wine seemed to have left her body, she wanted to replace it with food, with vegetables and rice. "Lunch?" she said again, and pointed first to the restaurant and then to her stomach.

The boy nodded. Today he was wearing long blue surf shorts. He pulled a tank top over his head, and looked down at the words: MIAMI: CATCH A FISH, hoping Yvonne would approve. She smiled, and, satisfied, he put on his sandals. They were blue and said ROOSTER on the wide plastic straps that crossed over the tops of his small feet. The boy gestured to Yvonne that he'd like to put his shells in her bag.

"Certainly," she said, and opened the purse for him. He placed each one inside, gingerly. She liked that she was now both client and partner. He trusted her to carry his cargo.

Together they walked to the restaurant, which was only just beginning to fill. For the yachting crowd, it was still too early in the day for lunch. The waiter, a short man in a tight white T-shirt, sneered as he seated them by the bathroom. It was the same waiter who had given her an unpleasant look her first day at Knidos.

"Do you speak Turkish?" the waiter said to Yvonne,

knowing she did not.

Yvonne shook her head.

"You know he is the widow's grandson." His English was good, his demeanor unfriendly.

Yvonne knew nothing about the boy's family. "What? I don't know who . . ."

"The widow owns the chateau on the hill," said the waiter.

"The French-looking one? By the road?"

The waiter nodded. "The boy comes to visit her in the summers."

"Where's his home?" she said.

"Cappadocia," he said.

The boy looked up and said something—probably confirming he lived there. The waiter said something to him in return.

"Where's Cappadocia?" said Yvonne.

"Where the Mevlana is from," the waiter said.

Yvonne shook her head.

"But you must know Mevlana," said the waiter, his face pinched.

She shook her head again and looked at the menu. She wished he would bring their food and leave her alone with the boy.

"Nothing to drink?" said the waiter. He must have been accustomed to making his money serving drinks to the Europeans who came to shore from their yachts.

"Just coffee," said Yvonne.

"Nescafé," said the waiter.

"Sure," said Yvonne. The boy ordered an orange Fanta.

The boy: she didn't know his name. She would have to ask him when the waiter left. Suddenly her curiosity was so great she felt aware of its presence on her tongue, under her nails. What was his name? What would it be?

Seconds later the waiter returned with their drinks and a tray of small dishes, each covered with Saran wrap. Yvonne selected yogurt, spinach, dolmas, and eggplant. The boy picked out a few other vegetables Yvonne didn't recognize. The waiter placed each dish on the table, and then, after removing the Saran wrap, rolled and compressed each piece of plastic into tiny, firm balls.

"Enjoy," the waiter said to Yvonne, and then spat a few quick words to the boy. The boy said nothing in return. The waiter stalked off.

"What is your name?" she asked the boy.

He looked at her, puzzled.

"My name," she said, pointing at herself, "is Yvonne."

The boy repeated it. She liked the way it sounded coming out of his mouth. *Eve-on*. He placed the accent on the wrong syllable, and, in his doing so, she heard her name anew.

"And your name is . . ." said Yvonne.

"Ahmet," he said, pointing his thumb in the center of his boyish chest. Yvonne stared at his thumb's placement, just below "Miami" and above "Catch a Fish." It was as though he was saying everything about him centered in that spot, everything he was emanated from there.

"Nice to meet you," said Yvonne.

"Nice to meet you," Ahmet repeated.

Yvonne couldn't tell if he knew more English than he was letting on, or if he was simply imitating her. She tried in vain to fan herself with a laminated drinks menu that remained on the table.

Ahmet was facing the ruins of Knidos, and his dark eyes traveled up to the top of the hill. Yvonne turned to see what had caught his attention: a man and a woman standing by a broken Ionic column, trying to wave to passengers on a boat down below them.

"Have you been there?" she asked Ahmet.

The boy shrugged.

Yvonne repeated herself, speaking slower this time and pointing.

The boy shook his head, now understanding.

Yvonne didn't want to give up his company. She didn't want to spend the afternoon on the beach alone, reading her book by herself.

"After lunch, you and me, we go?" she said, pointing to the two of them, and then the archaeological site.

"Yes?" said the boy.

"Yes."

The food was good, and Yvonne complimented Ahmet on his choices. They spent a good part of the meal looking at the couples being seated at adjacent tables, at the ocean, the sky.

A moment after she placed her fork and knife together at an angle across her plate, the waiter brought her the bill.

The boy said something to the waiter, and the waiter turned to Yvonne. His eyes narrowed in surprise. "So you are taking him to the ruins."

"He's never been there," Yvonne said.

"You know, the Aphrodite statue used to be there."

"Really?" Yvonne said.

"Some museums have copies of Aphrodite of Knidos. But no museum has the real one. It was destroyed by fire."

"That's too bad," Yvonne said.

"Yes," the waiter said. "I can see you would enjoy it."

Yvonne smiled, not knowing what to say. She didn't like this man.

"You're here in Turkey by yourself?"

"Yes."

"This is something women in America do? They come to a faraway country alone?"

Yvonne considered his question. She couldn't think of any of her friends who had made such a journey. Other women she knew traveled with a husband or a friend or a tour group. "Sure," she said.

He stood over them for too long, as if deciding what to say. Finally he chose his words. "I've known people like you," he said.

"And I've known people like you," Yvonne said, picturing the student who had written her the note about Cromwell. There had been such rage, such hatred contained inside his oblong Os. The waiter and Yvonne stared at each other until a fork dropped from a nearby table, and the waiter bent to retrieve it. With his dirty fork in hand, he scuttled off.

After Yvonne had settled the bill—she left a large tip meant to confound—she and Ahmet walked to the archaeological site. Near the entrance, a man and a woman sold tickets from a parked trailer, and Yvonne purchased two and handed them both to the boy. The tickets had pictures of the Knidos amphitheater, and Ahmet looked first at the pictures, then at the amphitheater behind the fence, and then back at the tickets. He seemed more excited about the pictures of the ruins than their physical presence.

"You can have them. They're for you," Yvonne said. Ahmet looked down at the tickets again before placing them in the pocket of his surf shorts. He walked carefully for a few steps, as though he didn't want to wrinkle them, and, after a minute, seemed to forget about them completely.

They paused in front of a large sign, written in Turkish on the left side and translated into English on the right.

Yvonne skimmed the sign. *Knidos was established on terraces that slope down to the sea . . . In the sixth century* B.C. *Knidos became a rich city . . . Knidos enjoyed its most brilliant time in the Hellenistic period (330–31* B.C.*) . . . In the seventh century* A.D., *as in the case of other coastal cities in Anatolia, Knidos fell prey to Arab raids from the sea. Evidence for this can be found in the Arabic inscriptions carved into the floor of one of the churches.*

Yvonne had not lately been interested in the distant past. Even the thought of ruins bored her. When she was done reading about Knidos, she looked at Ahmet to see if he was ready to ascend the hill of ruins. But he was still focused on the sign. When he was through, he looked at her and nodded.

They climbed the dusty path bordered on each side by white stone. Halfway up the hill, Ahmet picked up a foot-long cylindrical object that could have once been part of a column, or not—it was difficult to tell. He held it in his arms as if he was carrying a log.

"English what?" Ahmet said, lowering his chin to the stone.

"Ruins," said Yvonne, looking around. There were no guards here.

Ahmet tried to repeat the word back to her. He gestured at the hill around them, at the little that was left of what had once been a city.

"Rans," he said.

"History," she said, correcting herself. That would be an easier word to pronounce.

"History," said Ahmet with impressive ease.

"Good," she said instinctively.

Pride illuminated his face.

They reached the top terrace and Yvonne paused to catch her breath. There was no shade, but the breeze, when it came, brought with it the scent of a flower Yvonne didn't recognize. It had a sweet, doughy smell, like bread rising. She could see clearly down into the harbor. The masts of the ships looked taller from here, their white vertical lines segmenting the sky, like arms raised in toast. *Hear, hear! Well done!*

On the edge of the hill, she saw a stone structure that

looked promising. Anything that had a shape, that hadn't been destroyed, had potential. "Let's look over there," she said, and pointed.

Another sign explained that the stone object had once been a sundial. The boy read the description, his mouth moving silently. He turned to Yvonne and tapped his own wrist, where a watch would be if he'd been wearing one. Then he tapped the side of what remained of the sundial, as though trying to make it function once again. He said something and she understood him well enough to know he was saying *broken*. They both laughed, he at his own joke, and she at him, and then he appeared to laugh with joy because she understood him, understood he was amusing and smart. He skipped ahead of her on the path, and then veered away from it.

She had to hurry to catch up. She found him standing on one of the roofless and remaining walls of what could have once been a house, or a temple—the site was not marked. They weren't supposed to be here. As Yvonne came closer she saw that beneath and between the walls lay enormous pits.

"Careful," she said, and no more than a second had passed before Ahmet smiled and dropped into one.

Yvonne screamed.

A moment later, he reemerged intact—he had only jumped to a ledge a few feet down. He was a prankster.

"Okay, that's enough," Yvonne said. He had successfully

scared her, changed her mood. "Let's start heading down."

There was no shade to be found and the chirping of the insects in the bushes—the sound of heat itself—was making the walk unpleasant. Ahmet followed her, and then passed in front of her, leading the way. Yvonne had to be careful walking down the hill in her sandals—there were few stairs and the steep dirt paths provided little traction. But the boy in his plastic Roosters ran down the path with ease, small clouds of dust rising up in his wake.

The waiter was watching them from below, like a king surveying his small fiefdom. The boy had run past him, to the beach. But the waiter approached Yvonne as she reached the bottom of the path. "You two laugh and play like lovers," he said.

Yvonne stared at him. She didn't know why she had to explain herself. She had befriended a boy; the boy had befriended her. She continued walking toward the beach, where Ahmet stood, waiting for her. She waved enthusiastically, as though they hadn't seen each other in years.

In the late afternoon, after saying good-bye to Ahmet—they shook hands like business associates—Yvonne drove back to Datça, passing the hotel owned by Ahmet's grandmother. She wondered, for the first time, how Ahmet got from the hotel to the beach and back every day. Tomorrow she would offer him a ride. Tomorrow she would think of other activities for the two of them to do together. Simple things.

She turned the radio on, expecting the comedy show and its laugh track, but instead she found only Western pop music. She turned the radio off and opened all the windows.

Ahead of her, on the side of the road, she saw two figures swinging a third in a sheet. As in a gangster movie, they were going to throw the body off the cliff, dispose of it in the ocean below.

Yvonne stopped and put the car into reverse so she could see them better, and, more important, so they knew she was watching. The two men swinging the sheet placed it on the ground. A little girl emerged, laughing hysterically.

You old fool, Yvonne said to herself. She smiled and shrugged apologetically, then started the car and drove off.

Back in Datça, Yvonne parked, unlocked the gate, and climbed the stairs to the house. The door was open.

She stepped inside and saw a shape quickly swooping toward her. She ducked, and the shape passed. Yvonne had forgotten about the owl. With its wings spread the bird was enormous, much bigger than she would have imagined. It was circling the first floor. Suddenly it darted toward her and she ducked again, covering her hair with her hands, as it flew down the stairs to the basement, bumping into the wall and guardrail along the way.

Yvonne collapsed on a chair and pressed a hand to her heart, trying to stop its galloping.

She circled around the kitchen and living room. A roll

of paper towels and a small clock had been knocked to the ground. There were small brown pellets on the coffee table. She cleaned them off with a rag, which she discarded in the trash can.

The doorbell rang. Yvonne had left the door open, and before she reached it Özlem poked her head inside.

"Hi," Yvonne said. "I must look a mess. I—"

"You look good," Özlem said. "What is the word? Exuberant?"

"I don't think that's the word," Yvonne said, though she hoped it was.

"May I . . . ?"

"Sure," Yvonne said. "I'm sorry." She stepped away from the threshold with a theatrical curtsy, as though this could make up for her initial inhospitality. "I just got distracted. There was an owl here this morning when I woke up. It's still here."

"An owl? The bird?" Özlem asked.

"Yes."

"In the house or outside?"

"In the kitchen. I left the door open all morning, but he just went to the basement."

"It's still here?" Özlem confirmed.

Yvonne nodded.

Özlem was silent for a moment. "I think I know," she said cryptically.

"Did you just see it?" said Yvonne, looking toward the

stairway that led down below.

"No, but I saw it yesterday . . . or I saw its mate."

Yvonne looked at her.

"I didn't want to tell you yesterday because of the car."

Yvonne nodded.

"But yesterday I saw some children with . . . not a bow and arrow . . ." She gestured.

"A slingshot," Yvonne said, gesturing back.

"Yes, that. And I saw the animal fall from the tree."

"And then it came inside the house looking for shelter."

"No," Özlem said. "I'm sure it died. I know it died."

"How?"

"The kids went over and made sure it was dead. One of them took a feather and the other kids, they ran off screaming that he was dead."

"Maybe he was resting and came inside my house late last night."

"You don't know much about owls, do you?" Özlem said.

Yvonne had never thought much about owls before hearing their cries the first day in Datça as she walked on the promenade. Before then, she had thought they were exclusively nocturnal. She closed the door as though one might fly in as they spoke.

"They are . . . how do you say that they never leave their spouse? How do you say that they are what I am not?"

Yvonne turned back to Özlem, half expecting to see a smirk on her face. But the look on Özlem's face was one of utter devastation, of someone who was on the precipice of making a decision that she knew would ruin her. Yvonne had seen this expression on Aurelia's face too.

She stared at Özlem.

"Monotonous?" said Özlem.

"Monogamous?" Yvonne offered, slowly.

"Yes. Owls are that. And so I think what happened here is that the owl in your house came back looking for the owl that died—the mate."

Yvonne felt sick. "Do you want to sit down?" she said, needing to rest herself. She gestured toward a chair at the dining room table. She wanted to sit somewhere else for a change.

"The sun is there," said Özlem. "Let's sit on the couch. It was Ali's grandmother's, you know. I never wanted it in my house, but now I cannot see why I protest."

"I'll be right there," Yvonne said. "I need to wash my hands." She could smell the animal on her fingers. She scrubbed her hands, digging under her nails, and dried them thoroughly. Then she sat down on the armless chair across from the couch.

Özlem looked at Yvonne as if she had news to share.

"So you made your decision," Yvonne said.

"Yes," Özlem said. "I'm leaving Ali and going to live with my friend, who will leave his wife."

A gasp escaped Yvonne's lips. "I didn't know he was married."

"Yes, he has three children."

"Oh, Özlem!"

"But he doesn't love them."

"I see," said Yvonne, now more confused. Three children and he loved none of them.

"What do you think I must do?"

Yvonne paused. Her years of parenting, teaching, and friendship had taught her not to offer advice. She had learned that those who claimed they wanted it listened to it the least, and later resented her for giving it.

Özlem looked desperate. Even her hair seemed to have unleashed itself during their conversation. "Please, you must tell me. I cannot speak to anyone else about this. Please, what is your opinion?"

Yvonne spoke cautiously at first, but then the words came out in a rush. "I just don't know if you want to be *that* woman, do you?"

"What woman?"

"The kind of woman who does that." As Yvonne said this, she realized perhaps this was precisely the kind of woman that Özlem, with her high heels and sequined blouses and femme fatale demeanor, wanted to be.

Özlem shrugged. "It happened to me, it happens to her. Maybe she will do it to someone else."

"What do you think Ali will do when he finds out?" said Yvonne.

Özlem smiled. How impressed she seemed with herself.

"Oh, Özlem," Yvonne said. Her own voice sounded exasperated to her ears, but Özlem took her outburst as a sound of sympathy.

"I'll be okay. Don't worry," said Özlem.

"It's not that, it's just . . . you're breaking up a family."

"Ahhh," Özlem said, and the skin around the bridge of her nose seemed to tighten. "You are one of them. I forgot. Happy marriage. Yes, it makes sense."

"Whether I think you should go around breaking up other marriages has nothing to do with whether or not I had a happy marriage."

"It doesn't?" Özlem said.

Yvonne shook her head, suddenly unsure.

"You are all the same. You are so worried about your own marriages being broken up, you happy couples," said Özlem.

Yvonne wanted Özlem to leave. She was tired of young, self-centered women. Aurelia and Özlem, though different, shared a narcissism common to women in their twenties.

"But you're also selfish," Özlem said.

"*I'm selfish?*" Yvonne said. "How's that?"

"You think I can't have the chance to have what you have had. The opportunity. I am unhappy in my marriage and so is my lover. And you were happy with your . . . your Peter, but you don't want anyone else to have what you had."

"That's not true."

"Yes, it is," Özlem said. Instead of standing the way Aurelia did when challenging her mother, Özlem was relaxing into the couch. She was clearly enjoying herself. "You don't think others can find it if they don't find it the first time. It is only true love for you. Everything else is less important. You don't even want that for yourself again."

"Pardon?"

"You act like you are ninety. Like nothing will ever be as good. That is how smog you are about marriage."

"Smug," said Yvonne, and then was annoyed with herself for correcting Özlem.

They were silent for a minute.

"Why don't you say anything?" asked Özlem. Her face was contorted, excited.

"Because you have it all wrong."

"How?" Özlem said. She was now leaning forward on the edge of her seat. She was ready for a fight.

There was a part of Yvonne that didn't want to engage her—the same part that had always tried to duck Aurelia's accusations. For a long time Yvonne had been happy to let misconception remain as long as she didn't have to share the truth. But she had come to Datça to strip herself of these lies, to shed this grief. The grief and the lies were the same—one begot the other.

Yvonne wrapped her fingers around the base of the chair to steady herself, and started at the beginning. "I was closest to Aurelia when she was younger, because she was the one who needed me more. Her brother, her twin, was completely self-sufficient. From the time he started school, he was embraced by other kids, by other families even. Everyone loved Matthew."

As she heard herself speak, Yvonne feared she was telling the story too quickly, that she was rushing over the important facts and relevant observations, and providing useless ones. At the same time, she felt she couldn't say the words fast enough; she was eager for them to exist in the world.

She told Özlem about how Aurelia's troubles as a teen-ager had become a wedge in her marriage to Peter. How she knew Peter blamed Yvonne for their daughter's problems because Aurelia and Yvonne had always been close. Peter preferred to take responsibility for Matthew's successes.

When Aurelia was finished with rehab the first time, Peter didn't want her to come home right away. He wanted her to go to a school in Colorado that specialized in teenagers with addictions. But Yvonne was successful in her protests: Aurelia was their daughter, she argued, and she had given Yvonne tearful and convincing assurances that she would stay sober, that she was done with deception.

For a month after Aurelia returned home, Yvonne felt closer to her than ever before. On weekend mornings they hiked the Long Trail, and on weekday evenings they worked on putting up a trellis and planting jasmine in the backyard.

But then Aurelia started lying. She lied when she claimed she was vomiting from bad seafood she'd had at lunch. She lied every time she filled the O'Doul's bottles in the refrigerator with real beer. She lied every weekend when she put on her crisp white shirt and black skirt and said she was going to her hostessing job at Tortilla Flat. Yvonne discovered this lie when she decided to surprise her daughter one Friday night by visiting the restaurant with a few friends. When they showed up and Yvonne asked for Aurelia, the manager pulled her aside and told her that Aurelia had been fired two weeks before—she had been caught sipping tequila throughout her shift. Yvonne didn't tell her friends. She said it was her mistake, that Aurelia had mentioned she had the night off and, foolishly, Yvonne had forgotten. When Yvonne returned home she didn't tell Peter, either. She knew he would try to send Aurelia away again.

Soon, Yvonne found herself keeping other secrets from Peter. She saw the bruises on Aurelia's shins, from walking into bed frames and coffee tables while drunk, and told him nothing. She knew about Aurelia's brief flirtation with a muscle relaxer, some pills she'd gotten from a friend who worked at a drugstore; again she told Peter nothing. She began to resent Peter for making her tell all the lies, for forcing her to keep the burden of Aurelia to herself. In the twisted knot of sleepless nights Yvonne came to believe that Peter was fully aware of Aurelia's transgressions—how could he not be?—but that he'd decided that anything to do with Aurelia was Yvonne's responsibility.

"I don't know," Yvonne told Özlem, "I'm sorry to burden you with all of this. I must sound desperate—"

"No," Özlem said, firmly, and walked to the kitchen. She made tea and brought a damp hand towel to Yvonne. Confused, Yvonne used it to wipe her hands.

"For your eyes," Özlem explained. She retrieved the towel from Yvonne and rolled it up. "Here, lie down," she said, and placed it between Yvonne's forehead and nose.

The towel smelled like it had just been washed. It probably had been, Yvonne thought, remembering the maid. She shifted her head and the towel fell to the side. Özlem readjusted it.

Then Özlem sat by Yvonne's side, and Yvonne was thankful that she asked no more questions, that she was comfortable with silence. Finally, when Yvonne felt she had taken up enough of Özlem's time, she said, "You should go."

"Really? I think I should stay."

"You should go," Yvonne said. "I'll be fine."

"What about the owl?" Özlem asked, half joking.

"I'll deal with him," Yvonne said, intending to do nothing at all about the owl.

The next day was Friday, and Yvonne was supposed to be on the Knidos dock at ten for the trip to Cleopatra's Island. She awoke feeling good, relieved of a lie. Had she really told all that to Özlem?

She showered and washed her hair with mango shampoo she found in a bathroom cabinet. The lover's shampoo, she realized. Soaping her body, she wondered if her thighs and buttocks might have already firmed from her daily swims. She pulled on her swimsuit, the lining at the crotch and across her chest still slightly damp, and stepped into a light pink sundress—a gift from Aurelia. She faced her reflection. Her eyes—unswollen, thanks to Özlem's precautions— shone, and the combination of the dress and her days in the Knidos sun made her cheeks look pinched, her lips bright. She looked alive.

She ate cereal while standing at the sink. She presumed

the owl was still in the basement, but didn't want to check. With the sex swing on the third floor, it was only a matter of time, she thought, before each of the beds, seating areas, and rooms closed her out, and she would have to start living on the roof.

She left the front door open again, in case the owl wanted to leave, and locked the gate at the foot of the stairs. The air was cooler this early in the morning. She had a pleasant drive to Knidos, thinking about the day ahead. Deniz had said there would be an American couple on the boat and Yvonne briefly wondered about them before her mind turned to Ahmet. She rummaged through her purse as she drove. A few Turkish coins shifted around at the bottom—enough to buy a shell or two from the boy before she set out on the *gulet*.

Captain Galip was waiting for her on the dock. His hands were tucked into the pockets of his white Bermuda shorts. "*Merhaba*," he said, and offered a coarse hand to help her into the motorboat that would take them to *Deniz II*.

A minute after they pushed off, Yvonne realized she had not seen Ahmet. She turned to look for him and he was there, on the beach, alone. She waved and he did not wave back. Even from across the water that separated them, she believed she could make out the shape of his brow, his eyes. He was looking at her as though she had betrayed him by going on the boat, by not spending the day with him, and this caught Yvonne by surprise. *No!* she wanted to shout, first to him, and then to Captain Galip. Maybe she could return to Knidos, see Cleopatra's Island another day. She glanced at the Captain, his expression impenetrable beneath the dark shades of his sunglasses, and when she looked at the shore the boy was making his way to the other harbor, the harbor where she was not.

The motorboat pulled up to the side of *Deniz II*, where Deniz herself was standing at the top of the *gulet*'s ladder. "Please, you are welcome. I am so happy you come."

"Thank you," Yvonne said, hoisting herself up the ladder.

"Please," Deniz said, and directed her toward the back of the boat, where a man and a woman sat at a round table that appeared to have just been set for breakfast.

"Hello," said the man, standing.

"Good morning," said the woman, remaining seated.

"How are you?" Yvonne said, though it was clear they were both well. Better than well: their skin was bronze with sun and their chairs were pulled close to one another, as though magnetized. Both of them appeared to be around fifty, a few years younger than Yvonne.

"I'm Carol," said the woman.

"Jimson," said the man.

"Jimson?" said Yvonne.

He spelled it for her.

"I'm Yvonne."

Deniz turned her eyes to each person as they spoke. *Of course*, Yvonne thought, Deniz must have shepherded strangers together many times, and would be trying to determine if everyone would get along.

"Please," Deniz said to Yvonne, and directed her to sit at

the table, across from the tanned couple.

"Thank you," Yvonne said. She could see the ancient amphitheater from where she sat. She imagined it full, with hundreds of people watching her leave Ahmet. She told herself she had no obligation to the boy.

"Deniz says you're from Vermont," Jimson said. He said Deniz's name differently than Yvonne did, and she briefly wondered whose pronunciation was correct.

"Yes," she said. "Burlington."

"We're from Riverdale, just north of Manhattan," he said. His New York accent was stronger than Carol's.

"And you're here on . . ." Yvonne started. She had been about to say *your honeymoon*. Supposedly, the island they were going to visit had been given to Cleopatra by Marc Anthony on their honeymoon. The island's famous white sand had been brought over from Tunisia to satisfy the queen, the rumor went.

"We're here for the same reason everyone is," said Jimson, and then added, "Vacation."

Yvonne reminded herself that she was on vacation too.

"My grandparents were Turkish but I've never been here," Carol said.

Yvonne liked them. She liked their clear determination to enjoy their vacation together: it seemed oddly rare. More common were people who took satisfaction in not having a good time, who expected a country to prove it was deserving of the trouble it took to get there.

Deniz, who had been watching the conversation with a

mixture of skepticism and anticipation, must have decided that they were all getting along well enough. After asking what everyone would like to drink—"Please, you like coffee, tea?"—she retreated down the narrow staircase to the kitchen.

"Are you staying on a boat or in Datça or . . . ?" Yvonne was always surprised by her ability to make small talk. It came from years of teaching. All those parent-student conferences, all those exchanges with other teachers while standing by the oven-like warmth of the ever-failing photocopier.

"We're staying at a little chateau about ten miles from here," Carol said.

"Oh, the cute place with the parasols and pool," Yvonne said.

"It's nice," said Jimson. "It was owned by an Australian man—"

"Austrian," Carol interjected.

Jimson wasn't annoyed by the correction. "An Austrian man who died last year and now his widow, poor thing, is trying to keep it going."

Carol touched Jimson's elbow gently, and a look passed across both their faces, as though a shade had just been pulled down, or up.

My reputation precedes me, Yvonne thought. She could imagine Deniz briefing her passengers. *A nice widow from Vermont. She is a lovely widow.*

Yvonne was used to the passing discomfort Jimson and Carol were experiencing. She recognized their shared reaction from the times when the words *alcoholic* or *druggie* were spoken disparagingly in her presence, before the person speaking remembered that Yvonne's daughter was both. Yvonne would put on her best blank face—her mask—and nod, as though to say, *Keep going. If you gloss over this, I will support you in this endeavor, and we will continue talking as though nothing has happened, no insult delivered, no trespass made against my life. Keep talking, I beg you.*

"So what do you do in New York?" Yvonne asked.

Relief washed over Carol's face. She had good skin, the kind that didn't show wrinkles, and a delicate, pointed nose. "Jimson works in the city, in the jewelry business."

"I import diamonds," he said.

"Conflict-free ones," Carol added. "And I'm a designer." The pride with which she spoke suggested she was new at the job.

"What do you design?"

"Swimwear, swim cover-ups, anything to do with beaches," Carol said.

"Is that one of yours?" Yvonne said, looking at the caramel tunic she was wearing.

"It is! How did you know?"

"Isn't it spectacular," said Jimson, more as a statement than question.

"It is," Yvonne said, and then she answered Carol's question. "I knew because it looks like you."

Carol beamed. It was what every woman wanted, Yvonne thought, for the life around her—her clothes, her house, her car—to look like her, to be an extension of her.

"What about you?" said Jimson.

"I'm a teacher," Yvonne said.

"Oh, that's terrific," Carol said, as if grateful that Yvonne worked at all. A widowed homemaker, on the other hand— what would they talk about?

"Nice. Good for you," Jimson said.

Yvonne was used to this. All she had to do was state her profession and she received accolades. She could have taught basketball on unicycles, but it didn't matter as long as she was a teacher. As long as she was the mother of twins and taught, she was congratulated.

"So where were you before here?" Yvonne asked. Talk of teaching bored her. Teaching itself didn't bore her, her students didn't bore her, but vague talk about education seemed a waste of breath.

"We spent two days in Istanbul," Jimson said.

"So expensive!" said Carol.

"But we had a great time," said Jimson, squeezing something below the table—Carol's knee?

"I think I had a better time," Carol said, and laughed. She had full, red-painted lips that suggested sex. Yvonne looked down at her napkin.

"We went to the Cemberlitas," Carol said, looking at Yvonne as though she should know what this was.

Yvonne smiled, shook her head.

"It's this bathhouse that's supposed to be so great." She said its name again, as though repetition might trigger

Yvonne's memory.

Yvonne shook her head again.

"Well, I had the best massage," Carol said. "I mean, they really scrubbed me down."

"Your skin does look great," Yvonne said. It was true— she had noticed the skin on Carol's arms, polished and gleaming like a new trophy. "I don't know what it usually looks like, but it's glowing."

"That's what Jimson said!" Carol exclaimed. "Thank you."

"So she has this great time," Jimson said, "and I get an old man smelling of alcohol. Like he'd been bathing in it."

"Must have been raki," Yvonne said. It was the drink she and Peter had shared in Turkey all those years ago.

"What?"

"Raki. The Turkish liquor. Tastes like licorice."

Jimson pointed at Yvonne like she was onto something. He was a pointer.

"Meanwhile, the woman doing me could not have been sweeter or more attentive," Carol said.

"She did try to get your money with her sob story."

"That's true," said Carol. "Everyone in her life had died. Her mother was dead, her sisters were dead, her husband had died—"

Again, a dark look passed over both Jimson's and Carol's faces. Fortunately, they were all interrupted by one of the crewmen, the younger one who had a strong but not unpleasant body odor. He was wearing his white uniform again today—the white linen shorts and shirt with no undershirt—and had arrived at the table with coffee and an assortment of small white dishes. Yvonne's eyes passed over his offerings: creamy white yogurt, bread, honey, olives, eggs, and thick pieces of white feta cheese.

"Doesn't this look scrumptious?" Jimson said.

"It does," Yvonne said. If she had been alone she would have quickly devoured it all, but instead they each performed the dance of politely offering one another the food they themselves most coveted. "Cheese?" Yvonne said, holding it out to Carol and Jimson, before taking three thick slices for herself.

"This honey is to die for," Carol said, holding a spoonful out to Jimson so he could try it.

A loud mechanical sound erupted from below. Yvonne jumped. Lately, any sudden sound startled her.

"Anchor's going up," announced Jimson.

"We're off!" Carol said.

"Yvonne," Jimson said. "Would you mind taking a picture?"

"Not at all," Yvonne said, her heart still accelerating.

Jimson pulled out a small camera from his pocket and set it up for Yvonne before handing it across the table. The metal was still warm from his body. Carol removed Jimson's base-ball cap and he wiped a crumb from the side of her wide lips. They leaned in close to one another and smiled.

"Nice," Yvonne said.

"Take another," Carol said.

Through the lens she saw Knidos retreating in the back-ground. Jimson's and Carol's kind and exaggerated faces filled the frame.

"You look like honeymooners," Yvonne said.

"Twenty-one years ago we were," Carol said.

Jimson nodded. "We celebrated our twentieth last year in B.A."

"Buenos Aires," Carol clarified.

"Look at all those flags," Yvonne said. As they rounded the corner of Knidos, at the end of the Datça peninsula, there seemed to be Turkish flags everywhere, a dozen crescent moons.

Deniz was refilling their cups with coffee. "Everything is good? You like?" she said.

"Delicious," Yvonne said, and Deniz smiled the smile of someone who knew what the answer would be in advance, but still enjoyed hearing it.

"Why are there so many flags, Deniz?" said Carol.

Deniz looked up. "We are close to Greece," she said.

"Ah," Yvonne said. "Everyone likes to mark their terrain."

Yvonne hoped Deniz would sit so they could talk, but she turned toward the stairs and descended into the cabin.

There was more talk of Jimson and Carol's stay in Istanbul—the taxi driver who couldn't find the Blue Mosque, the unrelenting heat, the bridge over the Bosporus that alternated colors at night, the exorbitant price of Internet access at the Suisse Hotel. When there was a lull, Yvonne moved to the large cushioned seating area of the boat, just behind the table, and propped herself up with the large red, orange, and yellow chenille cushions. She opened her book so she would appear to be reading, but she listened to Jimson and Carol's chatter.

"Do you think Tessa would want one of the Turkish plates?" . . . "Do they hang things like that in dorm rooms? They don't frame posters they put up." . . . "I think she has a fridge in her room this year, but not a real kitchen."

Yvonne thought about how the meaningless talk between couples could fill days, years—an entire marriage. Sometimes it was the meaningless talk she missed most. She leaned over the back of the boat, studying the patterns of water in the wake. For a brief moment, Yvonne thought it was not impossible that she might meet a man one day and remarry. Then she exhaled sharply, extinguishing the thought as she would a candle.

From far away, Yvonne could see the famous beach, white as the moon. When they got close to shore, they nestled between two boats the same size as theirs. Yvonne felt the anchor drop; a moment later, she heard a splash. The younger crewman had jumped into the water and was swimming with his chin above the surface, the boat's line between his teeth. Deniz and Captain Galip yelled to him as he tried three times before successfully tying the rope to a boulder jutting from the shore.

"I guess I should go change into my swim trunks," Jimson said to Carol, before descending the stairs. "You?"

"I'm all set," Carol said. She pulled on the neck of her

tunic to reveal a bikini underneath.

The harbor was crowded with pleasure crafts. The yacht anchored to the right of *Deniz II* bore flags from several countries, as though it was trying to befriend everyone at sea. Yvonne heard splashes coming from near the *gulet* to their left. Two men had cannonballed into the water and were calling out to each other in English. Yvonne tried to place their accent—South African? Australian? The flag on the boat provided no assistance. It was a Turkish flag, a chartered boat.

"Hello," they called out. It took Carol and Yvonne a moment to realize the men were addressing them.

Carol waved.

"The water's great," said a man in blue swim trunks. "You should come in." British? Dutch?

"Maybe later," Carol said. "We just got here."

"Are you going to the island?"

New Zealanders, Yvonne decided, finally placing the accent.

"That's the plan," Carol said. "That's why we're here."

"You ladies should take a swim over here later for cocktails," said the other man, who was floating in an inner tube.

"Yeah, just use the password," said blue swim trunks.

"What's the password?" said Carol.

"Sex," Yvonne said, under her breath.

Carol laughed.

"Red wine," said the man in the inner tube.

"I thought you said to come for cocktails," Yvonne said.

"Ah, the woman in pink speaks," said the man in the

trunks.

"You're right," said the other man. "*Cock*tails is the password."

Jimson emerged from below, and upon seeing him, the men in the water stopped talking to the women and spoke more loudly to one another.

"Please," Deniz said. "You are ready?"

Jimson, Carol, and Yvonne looked at each other before nodding.

Captain Galip lowered the motorboat and took the three of them to the dock. He pointed to his watch to signal that he'd pick them up at five; they had three hours to explore the small island. From the dock, Yvonne could see that the white sand beach was roped off on all sides, like an artifact in a museum.

They walked single-file down the long, narrow dock, and, once they reached the island, followed a well-traveled dirt path.

"I saw some snakes," said an older British man as he passed Yvonne, on his way back to the dock. "Just so you know. Beware."

"Thank you," Yvonne said, unsure of what to do with the information. She would be staring at her feet all day.

"Should we explore the island before sitting down?" Carol said. "There's supposed to be an old amphitheater. You might like that, Yvonne."

Yvonne smiled, and Carol and Jimson took this for a *yes*. The problem with being a history teacher was that everyone assumed your interest in the past was undying. Every birthday gift was an antique.

They walked along the path, toward the sign that said AMPHITHEATER. The dirt path was spotted with holes made by animals.

"Watch where you step," Yvonne said. She had made a point of walking in front of Jimson and Carol. She was beginning to feel like their daughter, an only child on vacation with her parents, and she wanted to show them that they didn't need to babysit her. She had lost her husband, but that didn't make her a widow—not in the way most people pictured widows. She wasn't frail and easily duped; she wasn't weakhearted and dependent on others. She quickened her pace, as though escaping the expectations that clung to her.

"Hey, Speed Racer," Carol called. "Wait up."

The amphitheater looked like any other amphitheater. They paused in front of it for a moment, and Jimson asked Yvonne to take their picture. "Smile," she instructed, pointlessly: they were both inveterate smilers. They placed their cheeks close to each other and looked at the camera—the same pose Yvonne had seen them assume every time they had handed her the camera that day. Yvonne imagined what their photo albums must look like: pages of photos of the two of them, cheeks attached, in front of ever-changing backgrounds. They knew how to live, it seemed. Yvonne had intermittently known how to live too—had she not?

They continued down the path. The island was tiny. Already they were near the other side and could make out the blue ocean ahead of them.

"Look at that door," Carol said, pointing to a stone archway, the only remnant of a building that no longer existed.

"Door to nowhere," Yvonne said.

"Let me take your picture," Jimson said.

"I left my camera on the boat," Yvonne said. "I realized when we got to shore, but it's okay."

"I'll take it with my camera. We'll send you the picture."

"Okay," said Yvonne. She had few photos of herself since Peter's death. He had been the one who remembered to bring the camera.

She walked up the small incline to the doorway, stepped up onto the threshold, and screamed.

On the other side of the archway, just below her feet, a cliff dropped off to the blue water at least a hundred feet below. If she had gone any further, even if she had leaned forward, she would have fallen to her death.

"What is it?" Carol cried out.

"What happened?" Jimson said.

Yvonne, now standing in front of the arch, breathing, didn't move.

"Don't," she said to Jimson. He and Carol were standing on either side of her now, each of them with a protective hand on her shoulder. "You can peer over, but don't step up there," she said.

Jimson let go of her and approached the archway. "Outrageous," he said after looking through it. "You're kidding me."

"What is it?" Carol said.

"It just drops off. No warning, no rope. Nothing."

"We should say something," Carol said.

"To who?" Jimson said.

"I don't know. Someone on the island must be in charge."

"We should put a sign up," Yvonne said. Carol and Jimson nodded, but none of them had any paper or pens.

"Let's just block the path with rocks," Jimson said.

They all agreed this was a good idea, but five minutes into the project it seemed increasingly futile. The rocks weren't going to prevent anyone from approaching the door. They would have to build a wall to accomplish that.

"Maybe we tell someone," Jimson said, forgetting or choosing to forget that Carol had made that same proposal just minutes before.

They retraced their steps. Cicadas buzzed loudly, as though they too had grown agitated—as though they too felt menaced by the heat of the sun, the holes in the ground, the snakes.

Just above the beach, a few dozen wooden chaise longues and an occasional umbrella had been set up next to a small beverage stand. Men wearing Speedos spoke loudly on cell phones. Deeply tanned women adjusted the straps of their bikini tops or the thin necklacelike chains around their waists before closing their eyes and assenting to the sun.

Yvonne counted the couples. Eight sets, then nine. The couples by the beverage stand brought the number up to at least a dozen. What she was experiencing must be similar, she mused, to what a child-craving woman felt when passing a playground.

She sat down on a chaise longue near Carol and Jimson and opened her book, locating the place where she had left off. As she read about the young woman's sexual awakening, she felt a melting within her own body, between her legs and under her arms. The combination of the heat and the discoveries she had made at Mr. Çelik's house, and now the couples on the island, reminded her how long it had been since she had entertained the idea of sex. Certainly not when she was dating the ex-mayor, with the word-a-day vocabulary. Not since Peter.

She removed her sunglasses, the ridiculously large and purplish sunglasses she had paid too much for at duty-free in the Amsterdam airport, and closed her eyes. She felt beads of sweat between her lashes as she tried to remember what it had been like with Peter. From the start, sex between them had required little discussion or concern. There had been a pause in their intimacy during the years when they had been pushed apart, and when sex between them resumed, their bodies had aged. The backs of her thighs had started to sag, and his belly had grown first large and firm, and then shrunken and soft; they had politely and instinctually avoided these areas when touching each other.

In the months after Peter died, she had not been able to picture sex clearly, to remember twenty-six years of it. Now, as she leaned back on her elbows, with her eyes closed and her skin sweating in the sun, she could recall only a leg draped over hers, a wet mouth hot against her ear.

She told Jimson and Carol she was going for a swim. She hoped they wouldn't offer to join her, and they didn't. She walked down the wooden staircase that led to the water, the white sand beach to her right, blocked off and enticing.

The water was clear and she swam with her eyes open. When she emerged, she was out past the buoys. She laughed as she heard the splashes around her, the splashes caused by her own hands. She kicked harder with her feet and slapped at the water. She watched the ripples spread around her. She could see their boat, *Deniz II*, from afar. *How beautiful it is,* she thought. She felt a surge of happiness and gratitude. The cool water confirmed her existence, her power to propel herself, to stay afloat while below her was the unknown sea floor.

She swam back to shore and when she stood she felt the fineness of the sand on her feet. After searching for only a moment, she found a shell she thought Ahmet might like. It was coiled tightly on one end and opened like a trumpet on the other. Before stepping out of the water, she filled the shell with as much white sand as it would hold. Then she used the shower at the top of the stairs to rinse off, and joined Carol and Jimson on the chairs, where she watched the men in their small Speedos apply lotion, with slaps and caresses, to the backs of their companions.

◊ ◊ ◊

At five they returned to the boat. The water seemed rougher

now, and as Yvonne sat at the stern, she observed that the rocking of a boat wasn't side to side, like a cradle. It was more like a clock laid flat, tilting toward three, six, nine, and twelve before starting the cycle all over again.

At five-thirty Deniz emerged from below to squint at the sky, which had darkened. She yelled to Captain Galip and he came out and glared at the sky as well, and they exchanged what sounded like unhappy words. Deniz turned to her guests, smiled sweetly, and offered them cocktails. Jimson and Carol requested gin and tonics, Yvonne iced tea.

"Please," Deniz said, and gestured to the table, which had been set. "Please, we start eating now, and then we go to Knidos. The water become shaky."

"It does look like we'll be hitting some weather," Jimson said to Carol.

They settled into the same seats as they had taken at lunch, and the crewmen brought them their drinks. Carol took a long sip of her gin and tonic through a thin straw.

They ate quickly, and just after Deniz had followed the boys downstairs to wash the dishes, it began to rain. The sound of the drops on the tarp over the dinner table was loud, pellets thrown from the clouds.

"Something keeps hitting my leg," Carol said.

"They're small weights," Yvonne said. She had noticed them before—an assortment of ceramic fish, crabs, and anchor ornaments tied to the edges of the tablecloth to keep it from ballooning in the wind.

As if on cue, the wind suddenly grew stronger. Jimson,

Carol, and Yvonne pulled sweaters over their shoulders.

"Captain says you come down here," said Deniz, her head emerging from the stairway. She looked concerned.

They descended and Deniz led them into a bedroom. "I am sorry," she said. "There is no other place. Is better here."

"It's okay," Jimson and Carol said at the same time.

The room had two narrow beds. Jimson and Carol sat on one, Yvonne on the other. The rocking of the boat was more noticeable down below. Yvonne placed her hand against a wall.

"Are you looking forward to seeing your children next week?" Carol asked. Yvonne briefly wondered how they knew about her upcoming trip—had her reputation preceded her again?—before remembering she had mentioned it earlier in the day.

"Not if the weather's like this," she said.

Jimson laughed. "We had such a wonderful time visiting our daughter in Japan last year—she was studying there. Her junior year abroad."

Yvonne felt an emotion that it took her a moment to identify. Envy. Jimson and Carol had a daughter who made them unequivocally proud—a daughter they visited not at rehab centers with names like New Beginnings or Crossroads, but in a foreign country, where she was doing fine on her own. *A wonderful time visiting our daughter.* The words were so sweet, so impossible. Yvonne heard herself sigh. If a child was not strong, was not happy, did that mean the marriage was not strong or happy? Did the struggles of the child prove the failure of the marriage? Could the two threads ever be untangled?

From elsewhere on the boat came the sound of doors banging open and closed, followed by the sound of Deniz yelling at the boys. Windows and doors were promptly locked, with a suctioning sound that seemed to trap the three guests in an airtight hold.

"It'll be good to see my children," Yvonne said, finally. As she spoke, she was filled with the desire to have Matthew and Aurelia draped over her, as she had when they were young. So many Sunday mornings, there had been marathons, walkathons, fun runs, all passing by their house. Yvonne, Peter, and the twins would turn the couch to face the front window and lie together, eating oatmeal, counting blue caps and red shoes and see-through mesh shirts, happy they were together and unmoving, while the runners and walkers exhausted themselves just beyond the driveway.

"You're probably closer to them now than ever," Carol said. "We have a friend whose husband killed himself and the wife and the kids are like this . . ." She labored to entwine three fingers.

"Carol!" Jimson said.

"It's okay," Yvonne said.

She felt Jimson's and Carol's eyes upon her. "It wasn't a suicide," she said. "It was a car accident. A woman ran a red light and hit him."

"Oh my goodness," Carol gasped. "Were you in the car?"

"No," Yvonne said. "I was in the video store. Aurelia was

home visiting us from India, and . . ." There were too many details. Aurelia had come home from six months in India convinced she had healing powers. She'd stepped off the plane wearing an outfit of yellow silk (which, she told them, prevented her from absorbing the negative energy of others), and said she wanted to make amends.

The rocking of the boat was affecting Yvonne. All too soon, she was telling Carol and Jimson how Peter had been killed. She was telling them far too much. But she was unable to turn back.

She told them about how it started with Aurelia's visit. Their daughter had been out of their lives for a time, but now she was back from India, home for a week. She wanted to apologize, to spend the week repairing their relationship. "I know we can get back to a better place," was how she phrased it on the phone. *Such a strange way to put it*, Yvonne thought. Yvonne and Peter were reluctant to forgive her, afraid to invite chaos. "Please," Aurelia begged. "I'm different now." But the years had taught Peter and Yvonne to be suspicious. They were wary she would disappoint—or devastate—them again.

Aurelia arrived on a Sunday morning in spring, and by that evening Peter and Yvonne were looking for ways to slow the conversation. They didn't want to talk so much, afraid of what they might promise her, afraid they might forgive her fully if they weren't careful. It was Peter's idea to rent movies—"Ten, two for every night she's here."

"You don't think she'll accuse us of avoiding serious discussions?" Yvonne asked.

"We've had enough of those to last a lifetime," Peter said. He never said her name, as if the name alone caused the pain. Always it was *she* or *her*. Peter would ask what *she* had wanted when she called. Or he would detail a conversation with *another former friend of hers*. They always knew who they were talking about.

And so that evening Aurelia had stayed at home and Peter had dropped Yvonne off at the video store while he went down the street to pick up dinner. He would be back to get her in five minutes.

Yvonne had the ten movies and was walking out the door to look for Peter when she heard the high pitch of the bell as she stepped over the threshold. Then the moan of a horn. In the intersection she saw a large white car heading toward the driver's door of Peter's blue Honda. It was too close, too fast. She heard the screech of skidding tires, and then a hollow, tidy smack.

Yvonne ran to the passenger door of the Honda, opened it, and saw Peter's body contorted like a tangled puppet. She touched his forehead, warm with blood, and his wrist, broken and cold. She thought she saw his mouth move, but it was blood falling slowly from his chin. She wiped it off with the back of her hand.

"I'm here, I'm here," she said. "Peter. Say something."

She repeated his name, shaking his shoulder softly. The only logical thing was for him to sit back in his seat and say,

"Whoa, what a mess!" But he wasn't sitting back. He wasn't talking. She needed only to get him to talk. She touched his cheek, as if to begin the process, to lead his muscles to speak. Blood coursed from his mouth and over her fingers. "Peter!" A dozen people were watching now. She sensed someone trying to pull her away. "Peter!" She wanted him to begin talking so it would be she and him again. Not these people. If only he would speak, the two of them could talk about how terrifying the accident had been, how scared he was, and how Yvonne had seen it from the video store. "I saw the car coming toward you!" she would say. "You did?" Peter would say, his eyes open in his certain way, his way of expressing utter amazement at the things that could happen in life. "Oh my god, what a nightmare," he would say. But his mouth did not move.

Someone was dragging her away. She pulled herself free.

"Are you okay?" said a man.

"We've called an ambulance," said a woman.

The passenger-side window was gone.

"Is he okay?" said another voice.

"I wasn't in the car," Yvonne said. It was the only answer she thought to give. She turned again to Peter. "Speak!" She found herself tugging on his ear. She had done it occasionally when he wouldn't wake up after one of his afternoon naps. "Get up, get up!" She was screaming now.

Now a woman, *the woman*, the driver of the other car, was coming toward them. Yellow complexion, gray jeans.

She stood in front of their car, her arms extended, as though Peter was about to run her over. Broken glasses clutched in one hand, blood on her forehead. Not even enough to warrant stitches.

Yvonne stepped away from the car, but kept her hand on the handle of the passenger door. If she loosened her grip, it seemed, the car might disappear with Peter's body still inside. "What were you doing?" she screamed.

"I didn't see the light. I didn't see the light."

Yvonne stared at her, heaving. She recognized something in the woman's eyes, in her voice. She was high. *Of course*, Yvonne thought. She had spent so many hours thankful that at least Aurelia had never gotten a DUI or injured someone with her car. And now.

"I'm sorry," the woman said. "I have to go."

Yvonne heard something come from within her own voice—it was midway between a laugh and a growl. If the ambulance siren hadn't come then, drowning out the drum of her heart in her ears, she might have lunged at the woman with her yellow skin and tight jeans. Her car was a white monster, a shark. On the street lay its mangled license plate.

Yvonne walked toward the license plate instead of the woman. She picked it up and placed it under her arm. It was warm from the crash.

"You can't take that," the woman said.

"Sure I can," Yvonne hissed. She was convinced that if she worked hard enough, stared at this license plate intensely enough, its letters and numbers would produce a word, an answer, a meaning.

The paramedics tried to revive Peter before placing him on a gurney. As Yvonne rode in the ambulance, she held the license plate with one hand and Peter's hand in the other. His fingers felt broken, and this made her hold them harder, as though the warmth of her palm could meld them back together.

From inside, the cries of the ambulance were deafening. When they arrived at the emergency room, no one had to tell her anything. The doctor led her into a small room with an itchy couch and two boxes of tissues on the table and she knew.

After telling the story, Yvonne felt breathless, her lungs deflated. She had been amazed at what had come out of her mouth.

"Wow," Jimson said. "I'm so sorry."

"That is some story," Carol said, shaking her head, her lips open in disbelief. "You poor thing."

"What happened to the woman who hit him?" Jimson asked.

"She disappeared," Yvonne said. "She ran away from the scene of the accident. It was a rental car. She had lied and said she had insurance. She just left the car in the road and was gone."

"Just took off?" Carol said.

They were focusing on the wrong part of the story. Her husband had been killed and they were wondering what had happened to the drug-addled woman who had hit him.

"Happens all the time," Jimson said. "These hit-and-runs."

"That's why I think there should be cameras at every intersection," Carol said. "Then you catch the lady."

"But that's not feasible," said Jimson. "Think of the cost!"

"Well, at least she had the license plate," Carol said, as though Yvonne wasn't there. "That was smart."

Yvonne wasn't sure what kind of response she had wanted from them, but this wasn't it. There was a long pause.

"What do you think?" Carol said. "Do you want to go check with Deniz and see if it's alright for us to go up?"

"Yup, we should do that," Jimson said.

Yvonne felt petulant toward these people she had liked only minutes before. She excused herself to go to the bathroom, and sat on the closed seat of the toilet. The room was tiny, her knees and elbows touching the walls. She knew she wouldn't tell the story of Peter's death again. No response was adequate. The funeral should have taught her that.

It was late when they returned to Knidos. The rain had stopped and the night sky was brown. Deniz embraced each of them, nesting her hands to her heart after she had released them; she treated them all equally in her farewells. Captain Galip took Carol, Jimson, and Yvonne to shore on the motorboat. Everything was wet—the seats of the boat, the wind, Yvonne's hands and face.

"It was so great to meet you," said Jimson. Carol nodded enthusiastically.

Now they pity me, Yvonne thought. They would go back to the chateau and tell each other how lucky they were to have found each other, to still have one another, to have raised well-adjusted children whose lives rarely interrupted or questioned their own. Yvonne knew this because, in the beginning, she and Peter had done the same thing on many occasions. *This,* she thought, *was what the expression "love is blind" really meant: no couple wanted to believe there were millions just like them.*

"We should get your contact information," Carol said. The wind was blowing hard and for a moment Yvonne pretended she hadn't heard. They would exchange a few e-mails, and she would receive a holiday card from Jimson and Carol, their faces cheek-to-cheek. She already knew that in a year or two she would be removed from their mailing list. By then, they would have met other people on other trips, and their time on Cleopatra's Island, and her story of Peter's death, would blur into other stories they heard and movies they saw—if they remembered any detail at all.

Yvonne pretended to look for a pen. She knew she didn't have one. "Here," said Carol. "It's my card. For my clothing company, but you can find me this way."

On shore, Captain Galip turned to Carol and Jimson for payment, and Jimson produced an envelope, already prepared. Captain Galip peered inside and, without removing the money, shuffled through the bills with his thick fingers. When he was finished counting he nodded.

Then he turned to Yvonne.

It was a financial arrangement. When Deniz had asked her to come to the island, it had not been an invitation of friendship, but a business offer. Yvonne had not thought it through; she had not thought anything through. Fortunately, she still had money left over from her exchange in Istanbul, and it was all in her purse. She paid Captain Galip and gave him the coins she had intended to give Ahmet. "For the boys, the crewmen," she said, embarrassed. She knew it wasn't much.

Yvonne hugged Carol and Jimson and Captain Galip good-bye, wanting badly to be alone. She could see in their distracted eyes that they too were finished with the day, with the company they had kept. Yvonne looked briefly for Ahmet. He would not have dismissed her story of Peter's death, even if he couldn't understand it. He would have remained quiet, respectful, awed, devastated. She should have saved the story for him.

But there was no one at all at Knidos; the only two cars in the parking lot were the rentals belonging to her and to Carol and Jimson. She drove back to Datça in the dark and in the rain, which had started up again. At the house, there was a note from Özlem under the front door that said: "I stopped by to apologize."

Yvonne walked down to the basement to see if the owl had moved. It was sleeping on the top of a bookshelf, be-

tween a stack of CD cases and an old printer. She walked
back upstairs and turned on the television, and quickly grew
bored of an American show. She sorted through a deck of
playing cards; she had never learned how to play solitaire.
Hunger led her to the kitchen, where she saw the pomegranates she had bought a few days before. She sliced one in
half and removed and transferred the seeds into a bowl. She
ate a handful of seeds, and then another. She searched the
kitchen for more food. The tomatoes she had bought only
a few days before appeared to have shrunk away from their
skin, each the face of an old and toothless woman. She threw
them away and went to bed.

In the morning it was raining lightly, the sky the color of
driftwood. Yvonne felt she had to go to Knidos. She had to
see the boy. The look he had given her the day before, as he
watched her leave for Cleopatra's Island, haunted her. She
knew if she did not show up this would mean something to
him. He would feel abandoned or, worse, that he had never
been important to her.

As she walked out the door, she saw the maid coming up
the steps—hadn't she just come? Twice a week was too much.
She was wearing a different head scarf today, with bright yellow roses, and her husband and son were trailing behind her.
They each nodded hello to Yvonne, and she nodded back. A
moment later Yvonne heard a sound coming from within the
house. It was the owl. She covered her hair with her hands

as it flew over her head and out the door. A small flurry of black, like paper set to fire. The maid screamed. She pointed to the owl in the distance and said something to Yvonne. Then she held up her long skirt, turned, and ran down the stairs, back to the car she had come in. She was followed by her husband and her son. Yvonne ran after them.

"Come back," Yvonne said. "It's gone."

The husband was in the driver's seat already. Inside the car, the maid was crying or praying—Yvonne couldn't tell which. Maybe she was doing both. Did she think it was an omen? Yvonne watched the car drive off, and knew they would not return.

Yvonne locked up the house and drove. Knidos was as empty as it had been the night before. The restaurant was closed, the umbrellas pushed down as though in retreat from the sky. Yvonne held the shell she had taken from Cleopatra's Island.

She walked through the quiet harbor and toward the beach looking for Ahmet. She found no one but a lone fisherman. She walked to the other harbor, where only two boats remained, rocking visibly. The *Deniz II* had left.

On the beach she saw the boy, sitting alone, looking out at the boats. Relief passed through her, and she called to him. He turned in her direction and then turned back to the water. Yvonne approached him and seated herself beside him on a narrow log. The weight of her body rolled the log forward and the boy leaped up.

"Sorry," Yvonne said.

Ahmet's face was impenetrable.

"I brought you something," she said, and held out the shell.

The boy examined it.

"For you," she said.

He held it in his fingers, between the small half moons of his nails, and smiled.

"It's a terrible day," said Yvonne.

They both looked out at the water, at its gray and white foam. He nodded and smiled.

She realized she had nothing to offer him except companionship, and now she felt that was not enough. What interest could she hold for a boy of nine or ten? Her guilt—for leaving him the day before, for not knowing Turkish—prompted her to speak. "I'd like to commission you," she said. She knew he wouldn't understand, but she was still fashioning what it was she was offering.

"I pay you," she said, using accompanying hand gestures, "to bring me shells. Pretty shells from the ocean. I will pay you for your time. For every shell you bring me, I will give you money."

She explained her idea again, more slowly, and this time Ahmet appeared to understand. He smiled and extended his hand. She took it in her own—how cold his small fingers were—and lifted it up and down in an exaggerated handshake.

"Deal," she said.

"Deal," he repeated.

When Ahmet started walking to the water, she realized today was the first day she hadn't worn her swimsuit to Knidos. She had come to see the boy, not to swim.

"Are you sure you want to swim today?" she said, and looked up at the sky. "We can start tomorrow."

The boy stared at her, puzzled. Yvonne reminded herself that he wasn't a tourist in pursuit of a warm-weather dip and a tan. It was shells he sought, and the commission she had offered him for these shells. Cloudy skies meant nothing. She followed him to the edge of the water. She didn't want to be far from him.

Ahmet was intrepid. He walked only a few feet out into the ocean before hoisting the front of his body onto his bright white kickboard. The kickboard looked new, and because there were no stores in Knidos, and none Yvonne had seen in Yakaköy, she wondered if he had bought it in Datça. It was hard to picture him there, on the other side of the peninsula, in that other world.

She lifted her dress above her knees. The water was chilly but not as cold as she would have imagined. Ahmet would be warm enough, she thought, as she watched him kick his way out into the ocean.

He scooted himself forward on the kickboard so his head was over the front edge, and peered down into the water. Every few minutes he would leave the board and dive below. He spent twenty seconds or so underwater before emerging for breath. If his dive had been successful, he would place a shell into a small net tied to the front of the board.

The water today was rougher than usual. As Ahmet moved farther out into the ocean, Yvonne instinctually stepped forward into the water, as though there existed a string between them of finite length, and she could not let more distance expand between the two of them. A nervous feeling grew inside her stomach and her mind. *Relax*, she told herself.

An hour later, Ahmet returned to her, the kickboard in front of him, his legs scissoring behind. When he arrived on shore, he reached into the net and extracted three shells. One was smooth and fan-shaped, violet-colored. The second was pale blue, with a row of protruding quills. The third reminded her of a belly button.

"Beautiful," she said. She rummaged through her purse and found she had nothing to give him. Whatever money she had had, she'd handed to Captain Galip the evening before.

"Tomorrow I'll pay you your commission," she said. Guilt was balling up inside her again. "I promise."

He gave her a blank look of either trust or disbelief.

Yvonne saw the sand starting to darken and, a moment later, she felt drops of rain on her head. She offered Ahmet a ride home.

He placed the kickboard, his net, and his sandy towel in the trunk, so as not to dirty the car's interior—a polite gesture not everyone would have made, given the car's appearance. He buckled himself into the passenger seat, his legs not long enough to reach the floor. Yvonne tried to remember when Matthew had been that young, that small, and could not. When she tried to picture Matthew, she saw Ahmet instead.

She drove more carefully with Ahmet in the car. Alone, Yvonne felt invincible, but with the boy in the car, she gripped the wheel tightly and kept her eyes fixed on the road.

When they approached the chateau, the boy pointed. Yvonne pulled into the driveway and stopped the car to let him out. Ahmet signaled to her to open the trunk, which she did, and then he came around to the driver's side and pointed to her and then to the hotel. "You look," he said.

"Sure," she said. She felt oddly flattered that he wanted her to see his grandmother's hotel.

She followed the boy up the cement steps that led to more steps. By the entrance to each guest room sat an array of small rocks, painted with a room number and a flower or a moon. The rain was heavy and she saw no one. Carol and Jimson had said they were checking out early.

By the time they reached an open door, Yvonne was out of breath from the stairs. Inside, the smell of cooking greeted them from a warm kitchen. In the adjacent dining area, a man and a woman in their late thirties were listening to the radio and folding paper napkins into triangles.

Ahmet greeted them and they returned the greeting

without looking at him. Yvonne stood next to Ahmet for a moment in silence, watching the man and the woman fold the napkins, until the boy spoke again. She heard him say her name, the way he pronounced it. *Eve-on.* The man and the woman looked up from their work.

"*Merhaba,*" said the man.

"Hello," the woman said, and stood. "You are staying here?"

"*Merhaba,*" said Yvonne. "No, I'm just here with Ahmet."

"Oh," the woman said, and turned away, finished with Yvonne. In a glass case massage products were on display next to a price list. Yvonne guessed the woman served many roles at the hotel—cook, maid, masseuse. And she guessed the man, her boyfriend, most likely did maintenance.

On the walls, dozens of framed photos showed another couple: a handsome, white-haired man next to a dark-haired beauty. The boy's grandparents, Yvonne assumed.

"Is your grandmother here?" Yvonne asked Ahmet. She pointed to the woman in the picture.

He nodded, and she followed him to another room, an office. Inside, a woman was seated at a tidy desk with a glass of what looked like Scotch. The office seemed remarkably uncluttered, and it occurred to Yvonne that business at the chateau was probably not good.

The woman stood when Ahmet entered but she did not hug him, nor did he run to her. The medicinal smell of hard liquor hung in the room above them and between them.

"Hello," the grandmother said to Yvonne. She looked decades older than she had in the photos, though it was possible only a few years had passed. In her hand she held a pen with a large fake red flower on its cap. The glass before her, a finger of Scotch left, had been kissed many times—little lipstick was left on the grandmother's mouth.

Yvonne introduced herself.

"You are the one," the woman said. She had a thick accent.

"Excuse me?" said Yvonne.

"His good friend," said the grandmother.

"Yes," Yvonne said. She finally caught on that the woman did not seem to like her. "What has he said about me?" Yvonne was suddenly suspicious.

"Not him," the grandmother said, the flower on the pen shaking in her unsteady hand. "He says nothing. The waiter," the grandmother said. "In Knidos."

"Oh, I see," said Yvonne.

She wanted to leave. This was not the encounter she'd been expecting with Ahmet's grandmother. She had hoped they would exchange smiles over a cup of coffee, talk about the boy, how affable and enterprising he was. Instead, Yvonne now understood why he left the hotel each day for Knidos. The chateau was like a museum devoted to another, happier time. There was nothing here but sour regret.

"Well, it's lovely to meet you," Yvonne said. "I gave Ahmet a ride home, and I thought I'd say hello."

"And now you have," said the woman.

"Yes," said Yvonne. She wondered if it was the woman's

unfamiliarity with English that was causing a tonal problem. It wasn't, she decided, looking at the woman's unsmiling face.

"I'm a teacher back home," Yvonne said. "I have two children. They're coming this week."

"And before they get here you pretend he is your son."

Yvonne stood in silence. She forced a brief smile, said good-bye, and turned to the door. The grandmother said nothing.

Ahmet followed Yvonne down the stairs, a pleading look on his face. *Don't leave me here*, his eyes seemed to say. *Take me with you.*

"I'll see you tomorrow," she said, as cheerfully as she could.

The rain had lightened to a drizzle. Still, Yvonne drove back to Datça, with her body leaning close to the windshield, as though she were navigating her way through a torrential storm.

A woman was sitting on the covered patio of the Datça house, picking at a bug bite on her leg. It took Yvonne a moment to realize who it was.

"Özlem?" Yvonne said.

Özlem sat up, and instantly reconfigured her face into its usual presentable form. She seemed to exist as a beautiful creature only when viewed by someone else.

"How long have you been waiting out here?" Yvonne

asked, hearing the sound of rain hitting the patio roof.

She looked at the ambivalent gray sky and shrugged.

Yvonne unlocked the front door.

"Come in," she said. "Let's get you dry."

Özlem stepped inside, tentatively, and then gave up any air of hesitance and walked to the red spiral stairway. "Are her clothes still here?" she asked.

It took Yvonne a moment to understand.

"I think so," Yvonne said. "But you can borrow something of mine if you need to change." Now that they were inside, Yvonne saw Özlem's thin blouse was transparent with rain. She was shivering. "Let me help you. I'll bring you a towel. Do you want tea?"

"I need to see her things." Özlem placed her hand on the red railing and started up the stairs with a surge of energy that surprised Yvonne. She skipped a stair with each step.

When Yvonne caught up, Özlem was standing in front of the closet in the master bedroom. She had quickly figured out which side of the closet was Yvonne's and which side was the mistress's, and was examining each item of clothing before tugging it off the hanger, dropping it to the floor.

"Please stop," said Yvonne.

But Özlem continued to pull down all the clothes until there was nothing left on the mistress's side. Then she collapsed onto the floor, sobbing.

"I told him I was leaving," she said. "And he doesn't care. He almost seemed pleased. 'Now I can be with Manon,' he said."

"Manon?" Yvonne said.

Özlem sobbed again, as though the word *Manon* was the insult. "The French slut. Do you see her ugly prostitute clothes?"

Yvonne hadn't noticed anything unusual about the clothes in the closet. They appeared to be tasteful items in muted colors. If anything, they were the antithesis of the see-through blouses and short dresses Özlem preferred.

"Liar—he is a liar," Özlem said. "It's because she's French that he loves her, you know that, right?"

"I know nothing," Yvonne said. The truth of this statement hit her a moment after she'd said it.

"He makes fun of the French, but his whole life he has been secretly embarrassed to be Turkish. He wants to be European. He would deny it but—"

"Why don't we go downstairs?" Yvonne said. She wanted Özlem back on the ground floor. On the couch or the porch. Not here.

"I want to see the rest of the house," Özlem said. Her face was swollen, her mouth pouting. She looked like a little girl recovering from a tantrum.

Yvonne led the way, walking into the hallway. When she didn't hear footsteps behind her, she turned. Özlem was at the foot of the bed in the master bedroom, staring up at the ceiling. The hook. She was shaking her head, disgusted.

"Come on, Özlem," Yvonne said. "Why don't I draw you

a bath? It will warm you, calm you down."

Özlem was still staring at the hook. She was sputtering words in Turkish.

"I'm going to get a bath ready for you," Yvonne said again. She wanted Özlem contained.

She moved into the bathroom and was adjusting the water's temperature when Özlem came in. Her eyes were intense, focused. "Have you seen anything hanging from the ceiling in there?" asked Özlem.

Yvonne looked her in the eye, and said, "No."

"No?"

"You mean like a plant?"

Özlem shook her head, and a moment later she looked relieved. "Never mind. Do not regard what I say. I'm very fatigued."

Yvonne searched the cabinet beneath the sink and discovered liquid bath soap, which she poured into the tub. As she put the top back on, she held the bottle out to Özlem. "Look, it's Dove!"

Özlem's mouth was still for a moment. Then she burst into grateful laughter.

While Özlem bathed, Yvonne checked her e-mail downstairs. She cocked her head to listen for sounds that Özlem was done with her bath. If Özlem were to find the swing, or any of the photos, Yvonne didn't know what sort of state she might devolve into.

There was an e-mail from Aurelia. The subject header

asked, *"Where are you?"*

Yvonne hesitated before clicking. She read the note from Aurelia the way she had grown accustomed to reading every correspondence from her: with one eye turned away, in fear of what she might learn.

> *Hi Mom,*
>
> *I hope you're enjoying your time alone. I was thinking that you might be lonely. I am. Henry and I broke up (long story, I'll tell you later but believe it or not I am OKAY!). I'm not on the boat from Greece with the others. I thought I'd feel too alone without you OR Henry there. So I was thinking I'd spend a couple days before we all meet in Datça with you instead. I'll come to wherever you are. But where, exactly, are you? Let me know as soon as possible. My flight leaves on Tuesday and I changed it so I'll fly into Istanbul and will spend the night there. But I need to make plans for afterward. Does your cell phone really not work there?*
>
> *xoA*

Yvonne tried to figure out what day it was. Saturday? Despite Aurelia's assurance that she was fine, Yvonne didn't believe it. At best, the *okay* stage would last a day or two. She pictured Aurelia's face—her eyes, her mouth. No one had prepared her for this pull, strong as an undertow, between mother and daughter. It didn't matter what Aurelia had done or was going through—there was never a time when Yvonne didn't want to see her daughter, didn't want to lie next to her, whispering and wondering aloud.

Yvonne walked upstairs toward the bathroom door, which was ajar. The tub was empty. She entered the master bedroom, and then the closet—she expected she would see Özlem there, rummaging through the lover's clothes once more. But the clothes were on the floor, in the same disarray she had left them.

"Özlem," she said. The house was darkening earlier than usual. Through the windows the rain was diagonal, a thousand silver arrows.

Özlem wasn't in the bedrooms or bathrooms, and she couldn't have come downstairs without Yvonne noticing. There was only one other place—the third floor. Yvonne climbed the spiral staircase.

Özlem was sitting with her arms around her knees. The towel that had been wrapped around her was now unfastened so one breast was revealed. She was seated before the open trunk, staring. The sex swing.

"Do you want me to bring you some clothes?" Yvonne said, pretending she didn't know what was inside. These were two of her strengths: changing the subject and feigning ignorance.

"I'm going to leave Ali," Özlem said.

Yvonne nodded. She thought Özlem had already made this decision, but now, seeing her like this and hearing her say it in that tone, she understood that Özlem had not meant it before.

"I'm going to get my things tomorrow," Özlem said. "Do you think I could pass the night here?"

"Of course," Yvonne said.

Özlem pulled the towel around her torso and stood. With her bare foot, her painted toes, she closed the lid to the trunk.

They ate dinner and Yvonne tried to distract her. "My daughter is coming to visit," she said. She heard excitement in her own voice. "It's too bad you'll miss her."

"Yes, too bad," Özlem said, convincingly.

"She's flying to Istanbul and then coming here. Is there something I should tell her to see when she's there?"

"Give her my number in Istanbul," Özlem said. "She can call me." She wrote down the number and made Yvonne promise to give it to Aurelia.

There was the question of which room Özlem would sleep in—she didn't want the master bedroom below the hook. She settled on the room with the twin beds, and Yvonne didn't admit that this was the room in which she herself had been sleeping.

After Özlem had gone to bed, Yvonne sat on the master bed with her laptop. She wrote Aurelia. "Yes, please come," she typed, and gave her the address and phone number to the house, and Özlem's phone number in Istanbul. "Call her

if you need something," Yvonne wrote. "She's a good friend."
She began writing something about how sad she was about the
breakup with Henry and then deleted what she had written.

She turned off the lights and got under the covers. *I am
the mother of whatever household I enter,* she thought. It was
her role tonight, as Özlem slept in the twin bed, and it would
be her role again in a few days' time when Aurelia would ar-
rive, fresh from heartache and whatever else.

The next morning, the sun, looking pale, reappeared.
Yvonne went to the kitchen and started the coffeemaker. She
listened for Özlem, but heard nothing. After an hour, she
knocked on the door to the room where Özlem had slept,
and when she received no answer, she slowly opened it.
Özlem was gone.

Yvonne pulled on her swimsuit and the turquoise sundress,
packed her bag, and removed the euros she had hidden in the
raincoat pocket on her first day. It was windy out, the sun
not yet hot. She needed to see Ahmet. She worried he was
upset with her. She needed him to know she would pay him
the commission she had promised.

She descended into the bay at Knidos and parked. No
sign of the boy. She walked toward the beach, passing a family of four, Turkish tourists on their way back to the road.
The young girl was naked and covered in sand. The parents
were bickering, perhaps about how she had gotten that way.

Yvonne looked up and saw him. Ahmet was on the beach,

wearing a different set of swim trunks today. Red. He was squatting by the edge of the water, making some sort of structure out of the small sticks and debris that had been deposited by the waves.

She was so happy to see him she jogged to him, and almost hugged him hello. She composed herself.

"What are you building?" she asked him.

He looked up to her, and as though he had been waiting for her and for this very question, he began trampling over his construction, kicking the small branches and rocks in all directions. When he was finished, Ahmet looked up at the archaeological site on the hill, and then back down to his feet. "History," he said, smiling and pointing.

She nodded, understanding that he was using a word she had taught him. She laughed. He was a smart one. She pictured him a little older, and in her class. He would be the kind of student who would keep in touch after leaving Burlington High. For years she had kept a shelf in her office to display the accomplishments and correspondences of former students, but, save for a handful of postcards, a bound thesis about female knitters in literature, and a book about the Civil War written by a student who had transferred out of her class, it had remained disappointingly bare. She had recently placed three small cacti on the shelf instead.

"I brought you something," she said, and she removed the crisp new euros from her purse. "Your commission," she said. She paid him more than she had planned, more than he could have expected. But he did not look surprised. Instead, he took the money solemnly, as though he now had an enormous task before him. She considered asking for some of the money back to ease his burden. She should have known he was the kind of boy who would live up to whatever expectation he felt was placed on him.

He rolled the money like a cigarette and buried it beneath his towel. He looked around the beach to see if anyone was looking. Now that the sun had shown itself again, Knidos was filled with people. There was still a strong wind—the boats were rocking, their masts waving to and fro like errant compass arrows—but no one wanted to spend another day inside.

"I look," Ahmet said, and he walked into the ocean with his kickboard. Once he reached water that was deep enough, he scooted his stomach onto the board and set out, away from Yvonne. She watched him paddle with his small arms. He was exploring a different area today, closer to the rocks. To see him better, Yvonne walked down the beach, maybe fifteen feet further than she'd ventured before, and took a few steps into the water. She hadn't wanted him to leave her so fast.

The floor of the ocean was different here, more difficult to navigate with its sharp rocks and slippery weeds. The water was up to her calves, and she took a step in the direction of the boy. Her foot! A crab, a jellyfish. Or a piece of glass. The pain pinched and she leaped away from it and hobbled back to shore so she could examine her toe. She sat on the edge of the ocean, the tide making its sizzling sound before retracting, and cradled her foot in one hand.

With her other hand she spread her toes to assess the damage. A twig had lodged itself in the delicate space between her fourth and fifth toes. She removed the wood, and a small red dot of blood spread into a wider circle. She applied pressure with her fingers, and then looked up and out into the water.

She couldn't see the boy. She nursed her foot for another minute, and looked up again, this time fully expecting to see him paddling back to her. She stared at the dramatic rocking of the boats. The water was louder today. She looked toward the rocks. Surely his red swim trunks would stand out; surely she would be able to see them. Or at least his kickboard, which always remained on the surface even when he dove down below. But she saw nothing.

She moved slowly at first and then quickly, leaping into the water. Her foot pulsed with pain. Then she stood still, waiting for him to reemerge. She counted to ten. She counted to twenty. She adjusted her gaze to see farther out and then closer to shore.

He was playing a joke. He was demonstrating how long he could hold his breath. Or he had swum to a boat, and was hiding behind it.

Already she wanted to yell at him for this prank. She knew she would find him and would want to grab his arm and tell him how hurtful such jokes were.

Where was he?

She dove into the water, her dress twisting itself around

her legs. She stood on tiptoe where her feet could reach the bottom and pulled the dress off over her head, leaving it in the water to float or sink, and continued to swim out to where she had last seen the boy.

She got to where he had last been, but she saw nothing. Treading water, she looked around, her legs beating beneath her. She tried to see below the surface. The water was as thick as marble. "Ahmet!" she screamed. "Ahmet!" The panic in her own voice was frightening her.

"Ahmet," she called again more casually, as though she were summoning him to the dinner table. "Ahmet." The boats were to her left, the rocks to her right. She saw no sign of him in between.

By this point others on the beach and on the boats had taken notice of Yvonne's panic. A few men had jumped off boats in the harbor, one with a life preserver in hand. Some had left their chairs at the restaurant to come out to the dock. Yvonne appealed to all of them now instead of to Ahmet. "Help!" she screamed. "A boy! A boy!"

She swam diagonally to the left and then to the right, plunging her head below the surface every few strokes. But underwater, she could only see a few feet in front of her. She kicked with her legs, hoping she would touch a foot, a finger.

She screamed to everyone on shore. "A boy! A boy! Find the boy!"

More men and women jumped in and swam to her. Maybe he had gotten trapped in the weeds below. If she could only feel some part of his small body, she could dive down, untangle him.

She was thankful now to be surrounded by others—by men swimming, by a small fishing boat. She was growing weak. She needed them. Everyone tried to speak to her in Turkish, except for one man who spoke in Spanish. She told him that the boy was ten, that he was diving for shells. Suddenly she felt something against her leg and hope blossomed inside her, until she understood that one of the men diving underwater had encountered her calf. He swam to the surface, disappointed to see Yvonne's face.

Now the others were getting in the way. The splashing! Yvonne was afraid none of them would find him. She couldn't tell how much time had elapsed—three minutes, or thirty.

"Ahmet!" she yelled as she swam among and around the rocks. The water was rougher here, and she looked to see who could help her if she needed it. Many of the swimmers had now turned their attention to the docked boats, and were yelling up to the passengers, confirming, Yvonne assumed, that no boy had climbed aboard.

She turned her eyes to the rocks and there she saw something. The kickboard. It was knocking against the rocks, each wave turning it round and round, like the hand of a clock.

◇ ◇ ◇

Yvonne sat upright in the basement of the Datça house, five

towels pulled around her, shivering. She sat on a musty circular rug, in the dark.

The fishing boat had rescued her. The current had pulled her toward the rocks, and two or three men had hoisted her up onto the boat. There had been so many hands upon her, under her armpits, her knees.

When they arrived at the dock a crowd had gathered there, and on the beach. They were looking at her the way bystanders had after Peter's accident. They thought it was her son who had drowned.

But then there were others, the waiter among them. They looked at her as if she had submerged the boy with her own hands, her own weight.

She had swallowed so much salt water. Someone gave her a thermos of tea, which she drank in small sips.

She looked around for someone asking questions. She didn't know whom she was searching for—someone official. There were no ambulances or lifeguards. A boy had drowned and—

She spat out the tea in her mouth and vomit followed. It was pink and sinewy and attached itself to her hair. It covered her feet.

The fisherman was wearing a bandanna around his neck, and he handed it to Yvonne. But the smell of fish, and the man's sweat, made her vomit again. She looked up and saw faces staring at her as she stood in front of the amphitheater, vomiting onto the sandy white path.

How long had she stood there, bent over, while they

watched? How long had they watched without coming to her side? It might have been an hour. She didn't want to consider that less time could have passed before she walked to her car.

She had waited in her car. Doors closed, air-conditioning on. She waited with the engine running for five minutes, ten. She expected someone to come and question her, someone to come and stop her, arrest her, admonish her, punish her, scream.

But no one did. They had all watched her vomit, walk to her car, and sit in the parking lot, and no one had done a thing.

Even the fisherman who had rescued her and left her with his bandanna had returned to his boat.

She had known when she was doing it that walking to her car might not be the right thing to do. She knew she might regret it. But the limbo, where no one was accusing or assisting her, had made things worse. Her brain seemed to be swelling in the heat. She cradled her head in her hands.

She needed to go to Datça and think. She needed to be away from the sun, the stares. She needed cold water, shade. She needed stillness, the fortress of the house. She would go and think and come back. She waited for someone to stop her. She waited for someone to come running to the car and say the boy had been found. He was found and alive.

She waited but no one came.

When she got back to the house, she didn't remember

driving there.

Inside the house she still felt trapped. Even the sun, usually meek through the windows, felt accusatory. She made her way to the basement. The pungent scent of the owl still lingered.

She needed to think clearly. *Think*, she told herself. She knew she only had a limited amount of time to set things right. She had left Knidos without a word. That had been a mistake—she knew it now. She had known it then. She had behaved the way someone guilty would behave.

But nothing had happened. He had gone into the water, paddled out, and then nothing. No sound. No splashing. No cries.

She had watched him step into the water, closer to the rocks than usual. She had stepped in too, following his lead. Then something had punctured her foot, and she had gone back to the beach. When she looked up, she hadn't seen him. How long had her eyes been averted?

She told herself it wasn't her money that had prompted him to swim farther out than usual. But she knew it was. She should have known better. She who had traveled widely, she who had never tried to bring attention to herself, to disrupt anyone around her with loud laughter or disrespect, had put too much pressure on a young boy. For shells. Shells that she had already known would end up back home in a drawer full of pencils and tape dispensers, or at the bottom of a fishbowl. The shells meant nothing to her. She had only wanted to please the boy.

No, she had only wanted him to like her, to love her. She had wanted him to look at her the way Matthew and Aurelia had when they were young. Before Aurelia began ignoring her, and Matthew gravitated toward any family but theirs.

Yvonne rocked herself forward and backward as she sat on the circular rug. Her arms were crossed in front of her body, each hand holding the corners of the towel. She was cold. She realized she was still wearing her swimsuit. She tried to pull it off, but it was wet and clung to her. She wrestled with it, twisting around on the floor, finally releasing herself. She lay on the rug, exhausted, naked.

It was possible, since his body had not emerged from the water, that Ahmet had landed on the rocks and climbed to the top of the small mountain. Maybe he had been entertained by the fuss everyone was making. *Yes*, Yvonne thought, *he was hiding up there, and the next day he would be at the beach, waiting for her as usual*. He was a smart boy.

She tried to keep this image in her head—of Ahmet the joker, the clever one, perched on the mountain. And she kept it for as long as she could before she began to replay the events of the day once more.

The answer would come to her. She was sure that if she didn't figure it out, she would go mad. Had a current taken him under and out? How long had the kickboard been circling against the rocks?

The sun dropped and she remained in the basement. She

knew if she went upstairs, the sensor would click the lights on. She didn't want passing cars to know anyone was home. No one could know she was there.

She slept on the couch in the basement, the towels pulled over her still-naked body.

At the first sign of light, she rose from the couch to dress. She had to go to Knidos to see if the boy was there, if his body had been found, if an investigation was under way. She wanted to make it clear she hadn't intended to flee. She drove to Knidos with the heater on. She could not get warm.

Only two other cars were in the parking lot—neither of them police. The water was calm today. Yvonne sat in the Renault. She looked toward the beach, where she expected to see yellow tape, some sign of police inquiry, but nothing was roped off. All was the same. She looked toward the mountain above the rocks, where she had tried to convince herself Ahmet had climbed. The mountain was white and still.

Her eyes continued scanning the beach for a sign. And then she saw it: something turquoise and familiar. Her dress. Someone had draped it over the railing of the restaurant's deck.

Yvonne stepped out of the car and hurried to it. It seemed like evidence—of what, she did not know. But she needed to claim it.

She walked toward the restaurant, her eyes still scanning the beach for a sign that something had happened. She approached the dress and was touched by how carefully it had been laid out to dry. *Whoever did this does not blame me,* she thought. *Whoever did this does not hate me.*

Emboldened by a stranger's kindness, she walked to the beach with the dress folded and tucked under her arm. No sign of anything.

Was it possible she had imagined it all? She felt her forehead. It was clammy and reassuring. She was not well. Perhaps it had been a hallucination, the result of a fever. She walked to the front of the log, to the site where the boy had placed his towel the day before. The towel was gone. A good sign, she decided. She knelt on the sand and dug for a minute. Nothing. Hope rose inside her. A hallucination, yes. Anything else was impossible. A boy drowning in the ocean where he swam every day? Impossible.

She moved a few inches over and dug another hole. Nothing but darker sand below. She tried a third time, halfheartedly, to search for any proof. She found it. A roll of euros. Fifty euros. Almost a hundred dollars. A ridiculous amount. Her disappointment blistered into rage.

She didn't know if she should rebury the money or take it with her. The dress, the money. It was all evidence against her. She took the roll and stuffed it into her pocket. She hurried back to the car.

A voice called out to her. "You come back," it said.

Yvonne turned. The waiter. He had a rag in his hand, a visor on his head.

"Did he go far enough for you?"

Yvonne said nothing.

"Ahmet told me you were his . . . how do you say? Patron? I'm wondering you think he went far enough for you?" He was walking quickly toward her.

"I didn't ask him to go," she said. "I didn't ask . . ."

"You didn't ask him anything, maybe."

Yvonne continued walking to her car. He walked parallel to her. "You don't think he wanted to impress you, American boss lady."

"I wasn't his boss," Yvonne said. "I'm not his boss."

"Just remember. Not all of us are so eager to be your friend," the waiter said, and stopped walking.

She was quivering when she reached the car. Once inside, she immediately locked the doors. Driving away, Yvonne periodically checked her rearview mirror to see if she was being followed. She vowed to herself she would stop at the hotel and tell Ahmet's grandmother the truth about what had happened. She would say she was sorry, that there was nothing she could have done. She had tried to save the boy.

As she slowed near the chateau, she saw two figures walking along the road turn to look in her direction. She recognized them: the man and the woman who had been folding napkins the day Ahmet had taken Yvonne to meet his grandmother. Their eyes met Yvonne's and she lifted her hand, not as much to wave as to say, *Yes, it's me. Here I am.* The woman's face hardened, and the man turned his gaze to the ground.

She stopped the car and the man and woman continued

to stand where they were without approaching Yvonne. Half a minute went by. The man, his eyes still averted, gestured to Yvonne to keep driving. He pointed to the road ahead of her. Now the woman waved her arms the way one would to a stray and bothersome dog. *Go on, go home.*

Yvonne drove quickly, swinging around the curves until she found herself behind a row of cars, driving slowly. She considered passing them, but the procession was ten cars deep. She forced herself to be calm, to not drive too close to the blue car in front of her. A sign had been tied with rope to its license plate. She should have learned a few words of Turkish. She should have made an effort.

The cars she was trailing were slow and close together. It was, she decided, a funeral procession. The man and the woman who worked at the hotel had been wearing dark clothes—funeral clothes. The boy's funeral.

She tried to recall what one did in a funeral procession. She turned on her headlights, and then turned them off. She wasn't sure if it was right for her to join. She remembered a story she'd read in a newspaper about a mother who had killed her daughter and then herself. They had separate funerals, and were buried in different graveyards. Murderer and victim were to be separated in death, and thereafter.

But she was not a murderer. She was a woman who had befriended a boy. She turned her headlights on again.

The driver in the car she was following met her eye in his rearview mirror, and signaled to the right. A moment later, he pulled over to the side of the road, leaving room for

Yvonne to park behind him. She followed his car. She felt ready to face any judgment.

She stepped out of the car as the man walked toward her. He was not wearing dark clothes. He was smiling and said something in Turkish.

Yvonne indicated that she didn't understand.

"You need something?" he said, and as he looked at her she saw concern spread across his face. She could only imagine what she looked like.

"No," said Yvonne.

"You turn your lights on," said the man. "I thinked you want something, you want me do something."

"Oh, no," said Yvonne. "I thought it was a funeral."

"A funeral?"

"Yes."

The man laughed. "It's my nephew's circumcision," he said. He pointed to the sign on his license plate, as though it would explain something to Yvonne. "We left the mosque and now we go to the party."

"Your nephew?" Yvonne said.

"Three nephews. The cousins—they all get circumcised together. They go on camel ride so they have a good memory, and then . . ." He made a snip-snip gesture and laughed.

"I'm sorry," Yvonne said. "I didn't know."

"It's alright," said the man. "You are good?"

Yvonne was not good. She tried to smile.

"You are good," he said. "Have a nice day."

◊ ◊ ◊

Outside the house in Datça, a figure was pacing. Özlem.

"Hello," Yvonne said as she walked up the steps. She was filled with relief at seeing a friend. Her only friend.

"Come," Özlem said. "Let's get inside."

Once they were in the house, Özlem locked the door.

"So you heard," Yvonne said.

"Oh, Yvonne," she said. "I'm so sorry."

"What did you hear?"

Özlem stared at Yvonne, as though debating whether or not to tell her.

"It's okay," Yvonne said. "I need to know. The thoughts going through my head can't be worse than what you're going to tell me."

"They say you were friends with the boy who drowned."

"So he did drown," Yvonne said. She was suddenly nauseous.

"Yes," Özlem said, pausing. "They think he hit his head on the rocks. Maybe he was stuck below on something. Maybe the motor of a boat. He is gone."

They were standing in the hallway. Yvonne sat on the floor. She buried her face in her arms, blocking out the light.

Yvonne felt Özlem's hand on her hair, stroking it. She tried to remember the last person who had done this. Her middle sister, at their mother's funeral, had tried to calm her, console her, by touching her hair.

"You didn't know," Özlem said.

Yvonne shook her head, her face still in the fold of her arms.

"I'm sorry," Özlem said.

Yvonne released her arms and looked up. "What did they say?" As she spoke, she grew concerned. She thought of the waiter in Knidos. Özlem looked at her, unwilling to speak. "Please," Yvonne said.

"Some people are confused why you come here by yourself, why you become friends with the boy."

"I'm not allowed to travel alone?" She was surprised by the sound of her own voice. It was deep, loud, ferocious.

"I'm just telling you what I have heard."

"I know," Yvonne said. "I'm sorry."

"They think you gave him money to die. They know your husband is dead too, so they think something . . . everyone is just confused."

Yvonne stood and walked into the living room, where she paced back and forth between the bookshelf and rifle display.

Özlem looked at her, then at the window. "I think you should be careful," she said. "When I came here, I saw a television news crew leaving."

Yvonne seated herself on the step between the hallway and the living room. "What should I do?"

Özlem responded quickly, as though she had given much thought to the question. "You need to leave," she said.

"And go where?" Yvonne thought of Matthew, his boat coming to pick her up any day. Was it tomorrow?

"Get out of the country. Go home. It makes no sense to stay here when things are the way they are."

"I can't just leave," Yvonne said. "That makes it look like I did something wrong." She pictured the woman who had killed Peter. Her pasty skin, her gray jeans. Her dulled eyes. The sight of her backing up from the scene of the crash, before she turned to run.

"And his family," Yvonne said, and covered her eyes again, this time with the palms of her hands. "I think I need to see his family." As soon as she said the words, she knew she'd made the decision. "Do you know anything about them?"

Özlem was silent. She knew.

"Please," Yvonne said. "Please."

"They're from Cappadocia," Özlem said. "From a small town in Cappadocia."

"What's the name of the town?" Yvonne said.

Özlem hesitated a moment, and then spoke reluctantly. "Ürgüp."

Yvonne asked her to spell it. Özlem removed a receipt from her purse. On the back of it she wrote down the name of Ahmet's town and his family name and handed it to Yvonne. Yvonne stared at the receipt. She hadn't known his last name. *Yildirm*.

"I think you're making a mistake," Özlem said. "If I were you, I would do what I'm doing. Just leave. Go home."

"You're going to Istanbul?"

"I'm flying this afternoon. I think it's hopeless for me to fix anything here. You should go home too."

There was no time for a proper good-bye. Özlem held Yvonne gently, seeming afraid that Yvonne would crumble under any pressure at all.

After Özlem left, Yvonne packed her bags quickly. She would drive to Cappadocia. She didn't know where it was or how long it would take, but she would get there. As she drove down the hill to the main street, she began to worry. What would people think when they realized she had left town altogether?

There was no choice: she would turn herself in. She had seen a police station on the main street of Datça. It was a sterile, solid building, with a dozen cars parked outside every time she drove by, as though the police force was so busy inside they could not leave.

She would go to the station and tell them what had happened. Surely someone there spoke English. She would tell them everything she knew about the boy, everything that had happened that day and on the previous days. She imagined a row of dough-faced policemen listening to her story. She would leave the decision to them.

She drove to the police station and parked in the front lot. She climbed the three steps to the building, and found herself face-to-face with a bust of someone whose name she didn't recognize. She was staring at it when a policeman with a mustache greeted her. "*Merhaba*," he said, and added something she could not understand.

"*Merhaba*," she said.

She heard someone yelling and peered down the corridor.

Holding cells lined the first floor, and the shouts of a prisoner had summoned no fewer than three guards with their batons lifted into the air like torches.

She turned back to the mustached policeman. He was staring at her, waiting for her to state the reason for her presence.

"Is there a bathroom here?" Yvonne asked him.

He didn't understand.

"WC?" she said.

He shook his head.

Say something, she told herself. *Confess.*

"Ah, there you are," said a voice behind her. She turned. It was Ali Çelik. "I saw your car outside," he said to Yvonne.

Then he spoke in Turkish to the officer, and the officer responded. Yvonne thought she heard the officer say *WC* before smiling. Ali smiled, then turned to Yvonne and frowned. "Should we go, then?" he said. He grabbed hold of her elbow and led her out the door.

"I'm sorry about the car," she said, not sure what he wanted from her.

"What were you doing there?" he asked, ignoring her apology.

"I don't know," Yvonne said. They were standing outside the station.

Ali stared at her. "Don't be foolish," he said.

"You know?" Yvonne said.

"Yes," Ali said. "Some reporters called my house, and I

was on my way to see you when I saw your car parked here."
He lifted his chin in the direction of the Renault. "Are you
crazy?" he said.

"I wasn't planning on—" Yvonne said, and stopped. She
didn't know what she had planned. "I was on my way to Cappadocia."

"Why?"

She told Ali that Ahmet was from the region, how she
wanted to go to his parents, to explain everything to them.
The sun was hot on her dark hair.

"I think that's brave of you," Ali said. Yvonne was surprised. She had expected him to have the same reaction as
Özlem. "Everyone needs to make amends," he said. "I'm
happy you think this way."

Yvonne was so grateful she almost cried.

"But it's too far for you to drive there. You're in no condi-
tion to drive." He looked at her then and looked away. She
wondered what he was seeing. "I'll take you to the bus station," he added. "Give me the keys."

Ali adjusted the driver's seat of the Renault before turning on the engine. He drove her to the small office at the bus
station, removed her suitcase from the car, and helped her
get a ticket. There was no direct bus to the boy's town. She
would travel to Konya first, spend the night, and the next day
go to Ürgüp.

Ali sat with her in the small, spare terminal. They had
nothing left to say to each other, and soon he stood. He

walked to the ticket office in the station and came back with
a small man in a uniform.

"This man will watch you now," Ali said.

"Thank you," Yvonne said, and took Ali's hand.

"Thank you for coming to Turkey," he said. He had adopted
a tone he might have used with anyone, any person who had
rented his home and was now departing. "I have enjoyed
meeting you." He squeezed her hand and let it drop. Then he
turned and disappeared out the door.

The man in uniform was the manager of the bus station. He
invited Yvonne into his office. "You shouldn't have to wait
out there," he said. She agreed to follow him. He pulled her
suitcase for her and dusted off a metal chair next to his desk.

He wanted to show off his English. He showed her pictures of his wife and son. "You go to Konya?" he said.

"I'm stopping there," said Yvonne.

"Konya is very religion," said the man. "The Mevlana is
in Konya."

"The Mevlana? I'm sorry."

"You don't know?"

"No."

"The Mevlana?"

"No," Yvonne said. She regretted coming into his office.

"Maybe it calls something else in English," he said, and
turned on his ancient computer, which made snoring sounds
while flashing a series of green lights.

He typed using only his two index fingers, and then gestured to the screen as though he had just performed a magic trick. "Rumi," he said. "That is what you call him."

Yvonne nodded. She knew the famous poet, had seen his books in the homes of her friends. "Okay, now I know," she said. She hoped that would end the conversation.

"I meet a woman once many years ago when I work in Istanbul. She is Londonish and she never come to Turkey before but she has a dream. In her dream she sees men in white hats spinning and spinning. So she visits the books to find answer to what are these men who spin. She finds they are dervishes in Konya. Her life is very difficult but she gets her money and leaves her husband and comes to Konya to see the men, and it is as in her dream. My friend thinks she is Muslim after that. She says she was saved."

He looked at Yvonne expectantly, as though she too harbored such dreams.

"I'm just passing through," Yvonne said. "I'm catching another bus there tomorrow morning."

"But you stay in Konya?"

"A night, yes," Yvonne said.

"Then you go see dervishes, and Mevlana's tomb. It is in Mevlana Museum."

Yvonne looked at her watch. Fifteen minutes until her bus left. She wanted to be on the bus before the police or the news reporters or anyone else discovered where she was. She wanted to go straight to Ahmet's family. They were the only ones who needed her explanation, the only ones who would be able to forgive or condemn her.

"Your bus is here," the man said.

The bus was large and white, a tour bus, though it appeared all the other people boarding were locals, some with their entire families—children and parents. She took a seat toward the back, next to the window, and forced herself to think about what she would say to Ahmet's family. She had no idea where she would start, or, it occurred to her, how she would find them.

A young man walked down the aisle of the bus offering coffee and food. When he reached Yvonne, she declined his offer of coffee—she was jittery enough—but accepted the fluorescent green package he was providing as a snack. Fruitcake. She nodded at the man to say thank you, and he smiled at her.

She tried to sleep but wasn't tired. She tried to read but felt carsick. She ripped open the fluorescent wrapper and ate the fruitcake in three bites. She looked out the window, watching intermittent signs for Konya. KONYA 310 KILOMETERS, KONYA 240 KILOMETERS.

The bus stopped at a small station. Yvonne used a restroom where she heard a woman vomiting in the next stall. In the small station store, Yvonne bought a bag of pretzel sticks and water, and then stood outside in the afternoon sun. She saw a group of policemen chatting in the shade. *Come and get me*, Yvonne thought. *Come and get me*, she thought as each car passed. Standing in the bright sun without sunglasses made Yvonne feel less guilty, less like a fugitive. *I'm here, right out in the open. Take me.*

As she reboarded the bus, she passed the woman who had vomited in the bathroom. The woman caught her eye and quickly looked away.

At the Konya bus station, Yvonne asked a taxi driver to take her to a hotel, any hotel.

The driver thought it over for a moment. "Hotel Mevlana," he said.

Yvonne rolled the window down. The fumes of the crowded city invaded the taxi, her nose. She concentrated on exhaling. Konya was composed of endless roundabouts crowded with hundreds of bikes and buses, and by the time they pulled up outside the Hotel Mevlana, Yvonne was dizzy from the turns, the heat. She paid the driver and circled through the revolving door of the hotel into the dark lobby. She checked in for the night and requested an early wake-up call; her bus to Ürgüp left at six-thirty in the morning.

She rode the elevator to the third floor and stepped out into a dark hallway. After a few steps, the lights sparked on and Yvonne jumped in surprise. Her room was also dark, until she inserted her room key into a slot. When the lights came on, so did the air-conditioning. The wallpaper in the room was gold, the bedspread a baptismal white.

She showered, washing the film of dirt from her body and face, and sat naked on the bed, waiting for coolness to settle into the room. Already she felt better to have escaped Datça, to have disappeared this much, this far. But thoughts of Ahmet quickly overwhelmed her. The faces all around her, splashing, yelling. She lay on the bed, feeling the man's hand on her leg underwater, the man who thought he had found Ahmet. She needed to leave the room. She could not be alone here.

She thought of the bus-station manager, his story about the woman who had been saved by the Mevlana and the dervishes. What had this woman seen? She dressed quickly and set out from the hotel with a map in her hands.

She reentered the hotel twice to get directions to the Mevlana Museum. "Right down the street," said the clerk the first time. The second time he pointed: "A white building." Embarrassed, Yvonne pretended she saw it in the distance and thanked him.

Each time she left the hotel, she pushed through the revolving doors, and each time she was assaulted by the heat and the smell of diesel. She left the hotel driveway and after two roundabouts she was lost again. There were no crosswalks anywhere in the city. The cars honked their horns and the bikes rang their bells. A family of four navigated through the traffic on a single bicycle, the father pedaling with one child on the handlebars, another child and the mother sitting behind him. She felt ill.

"Madame," called out men selling pizzas and plates and souvenirs with pictures of the Mevlana, a man in a white beard. "Madame, what are you looking for?" Yvonne continued walking. She seemed to be the only tourist in Konya.

Finally, she found the Mevlana Museum. Half a dozen guards stood talking or smoking at the entrance. She hurried inside.

All the women in the museum wore head scarves, each of them bright with floral patterns. She touched her own head, trying to imagine what it would feel like covered. Her fingers found her oversized duty-free sunglasses perched on her head, and she quickly removed and stashed them in her purse. She stopped, as instructed, by a bin that contained blue plastic bags and pulled them over her shoes.

She stepped into a crowded room. A mass of women were walking reverently in a circle around a glass case in the center of the room. Yvonne walked around them, trying to determine what it was they were circling. In the case she glimpsed a pearl-colored box, but what was inside the box was unclear. She watched the women place the fingers of both hands together, holding them close and lifting them, as though cupping water they were about to drink. They did this over and over again while they circled the small box.

When the crowd thinned momentarily, Yvonne approached the box. A plaque revealed its contents: THE BEARD OF MOHAMMED. Yvonne was dumbstruck. She had no idea that such an artifact existed. Was there anything like this in Christianity? What could approach this? The Shroud of Turin? The vial of Jesus' blood? She was envious of the women who could get so close to material evidence of their prophet.

A family began circling the box and Yvonne, feeling like an impostor, stepped out of the way. The father and mother were trailed by a young girl wearing a white dress patterned with pink sheep. The girl lifted her hands to her face, mimicking her parents. She caught Yvonne's eye and Yvonne looked away.

The girl, the heat, the circling. Yvonne needed air, then food. She needed to leave the museum. She walked past the guards before realizing the blue galoshes were still pulled over her sandals. She removed them quickly and left.

Water trickled loudly from a large, tiled fountain, with small stools around its shaded perimeter. Men were seated on some of the stools, using tin cups attached to the fountain with chains to drink and wash. Yvonne seated herself on one of the low stools, filled a tin cup from one of the spigots, and poured water on her feet. Then she filled the cup again and soaked her head. Water trickled down her back as she walked away. The coolness traveled through her.

There was no place to eat. From a street vendor she bought a vanilla ice cream bar coated in chocolate. She ate it quickly, messily, to keep it from melting in the heat. She ran across streets, relieved each time she made it to the sidewalk. In store windows she saw huge wedding photos, outsized funeral wreaths. Women in basements rolled dough on large, circular tables. In barbershops men were shaved while seated in gleaming orange-and-chrome chairs. She passed a white building with a strange sign: a smiling dolphin wearing a police uniform and riding a motorbike. She quickened her pace until she came to a street crowded with restaurants and students.

She paused in front of a shingled building that was labeled TEAHOUSE and listened to the music coming from within. It was the same music playing throughout Konya—wordless songs without beginning or end. A young man in the doorway of the teahouse called out to her.

"Madame," he said. "Your children. They are here."

Yvonne shook her head, but the man—the maître d'—pointed up to the roof of the teahouse.

"Yes, they are here," he said. "Upstairs."

It made no sense that her children would be here, but the man was so certain. Had her children come to Konya to surprise her? How could they know she was here?

"Follow me," the maître d' said, and because Yvonne was hungry and thirsty and because anything seemed possible, she followed the man as he led her up narrow stairs covered with broken tiles, past walls decorated with dull pewter plates. Her stomach spun and her breath was short. She felt she would collapse on her children when she saw them. Gratitude overcame her. She would tell them everything. She would tell them how sorry she was that everything was not as it should be.

Yvonne followed the maître d' onto the roof of the building, where students were talking animatedly in groups, or reading books alone. Yvonne scanned the tables, seeing girls in tight dresses and head scarves flirting with boys who took long inhalations from water pipes. She followed the man, her head turning everywhere, certain she would see her children before he did.

The maître d' paused in front of a table, where a young man and woman sat writing postcards. They were pale-skinned with dark blond hair. They were not her children.

"Here they are," the maître d' said. The couple looked up at Yvonne, confused. The young man looked sympathetic. "Long day?"

Yvonne could not speak. She closed her eyes.

"Where are you from?" the woman said.

"Canada," the man guessed.

"Netherlands," the woman said, pointing to herself and her companion.

"Apparently we're the only tourists in Konya not from Turkey," the man said, smiling up at Yvonne.

Yvonne was just beginning to regain her equilibrium.

The maître d' looked at the couple, and then at Yvonne. "No?"

"No," the young man said.

"Oh, madame, I am sorry," the maître d' said. And suddenly Yvonne felt he did have something to be sorry for. She had thought for a brief ridiculous moment that she would find her children here, that they would hold her this night, take care of her and let her fall apart between them. They would ride with her on the next bus, their shoulders against her shoulders as they traveled to Ürgüp, to Ahmet's family, to set things right.

Now she wanted to be away from this place.

Yvonne quickly descended the narrow, chipped steps, all the way down until she couldn't go any farther. But she had gone too far. She was in the basement of the teahouse, with couches and a barber's chair. The heavy scent of smoke and spice hung in the room. Though the room was empty, it still felt alive, as though a great number of people had congregated there the night before and departed in the early hours of morning.

Yvonne ran back up to the first floor of the teahouse, and then out onto the street. Something compelled her to look up at the roof, and she saw the two pale faces of the young couple who had been writing postcards. They were looking down at her, waiting to see where she would go. She walked quickly around the corner and continued past furniture stores with large gold beds on display, past cars and buses and bikes, the endless stream of traffic. Everyone in this city, it appeared, wanted to be someplace they were not.

Dusk was falling. She was so hungry.

She saw the mosque with its green tower and golden minaret and knew she was close to the Mevlana Museum and her hotel. She walked closer and saw men and women arriving at a restaurant by taxi. She followed them through the front doors and smelled hot food.

"You are here for dervishes?" said a man in the foyer. He was wearing a white button-down shirt with a beaded necklace and ironed jeans.

Yvonne shook her head. Then she said, "Maybe."

"There are a few more spaces. The performance is at eight o'clock."

"And I can eat before?"

The man smiled warmly and gestured upstairs. "Yes, it is included." He told her the price and she handed him the money.

"I'll see you in one hour, at eight o'clock," he said as he gestured once again to the stairs.

The restaurant was located on a roof with a view of the Mevlana Museum and the mosque. From somewhere—the rose garden below? the mosque?—came the sound of a flute. She closed her eyes and listened. She wanted to swim in the sound. She was so light-headed she felt she might faint.

She ordered *eski ebelli* because the menu said it was a specialty of Konya. When it came she saw it was a large round piece of dough with vegetables and meat wrapped inside. This was what all the women in Konya were making with their rolling pins.

She ate greedily, ravenously, pieces of meat dropping onto her plate. Oil oozed onto her hands. The small thin napkins on the table couldn't absorb the oil and her hands remained slippery. She hunched over her table so no one would be able to see the mess she was making, the grease on her face. She was the only person at the large restaurant who was dining alone.

After eating, she felt calm. The sound of the flute and the night breeze relaxed her. It was five minutes to eight, and she decided she would watch the performance for a few minutes. She thought of the woman who dreamt of the dervishes. She longed for distraction.

The performance room was filled with folding chairs and incense smoke. There was only one empty chair left, on the edge of the front row, waiting for her. She seated herself as silently as she could.

Four men dressed in white robes and tall narrow hats moved to the center of the room: the dervishes. They were in their forties, all dark-haired and with medium builds. At once, they all began to move. With one slippered foot anchoring them to the floor, the other foot performed an elaborate act of slowly pushing off from the floor and raising to the calf of the opposite leg, before lowering and pushing off once again. Soon they spun quickly, all in the same direction, in perfect unison. They appeared to enter a trancelike state, and the hands of their extended arms turned in opposite directions, one palm up, one down. Yvonne watched, mesmerized. She could feel the breeze created by the swirl of the dervishes' robes on her ankles.

Ten minutes passed, then fifteen. They were still circling in their own realm, equidistant from each other. Yvonne was beginning to get dizzy. She wondered how much longer she could watch the spinning. She wondered if they always turned in the same direction. A small part of her wanted one of them to fall, or at least open his eyes. Anything to break the relentlessness of the turning, turning, turning.

Finally she heard the padding of the right feet on the floor begin to slow, and she saw the dervishes were halting their private cyclones. The incense was stronger, and the room hotter, without the breeze from their robes. Yvonne stood and briskly made her way to the exit.

There was no taxi in sight, so she walked. She knew the Hotel Mevlana was close. She consulted her useless map and walked down a street that bordered a stone wall. Farther down the street the wall was lower, and she could see that it circumscribed a graveyard, crowded with tall, narrow tombstones the size and shape of grandfather clocks. She looked closely at one to read the dates, to see if the bodies were recent or ancient burials, and she took in a quick breath when she saw the name: AHMET.

She read the tombstone next to it: AHMET.

She clutched her purse and ran down the street toward the hotel. As she ran, she continued to look for names on the tombstones, and every other tombstone, it seemed, announced the death of Ahmet.

When she arrived at the end of the cemetery she was breathless. She looked up at where she thought the hotel would be, but there was only an empty gas station, now closed. She looked to her left and right. The only light came from cars as they sped past. She turned—she could retrace her steps, but that would mean passing the cemetery again. She was soaked in sweat. She felt hunted.

"Taxi," called a man, and Yvonne turned. "I take you," he said.

She had no choice. She followed him across the street and he asked where she was going. "Hotel Mevlana," she said. He pointed her to a yellow taxicab. She stepped into the backseat, and a moment later the front passenger door opened. Another man was getting inside. Yvonne looked at the driver, who didn't look at her. Instead he turned to his friend, who was lighting up a cigarette. She gripped her purse, ready to flee.

The driver said something that included *Hotel Mevlana*, and Yvonne tried to take relief in this. This wasn't an abduction; they would take her to her hotel after all. The taxi pulled out of the dark gas station and into the night, zooming past the cemetery. Yvonne kept her eyes on the backs of the men's heads. She could smell her own sweat—meaty and spicy and strange. She smelled like someone else.

When the taxi pulled up in front of her hotel, the meter read one amount and the driver quoted her a much larger one. She didn't want to argue. He had smelled her fear. She had arrived back at the hotel safe from cemeteries and the twirling of men. She paid him the extra amount he was charging, and ran out of the taxi and took the elevator to the third floor. The lights switched on, startling her as she scurried down the hall. She closed the door to her room, bolting and chaining it behind her.

She closed her eyes but did not sleep. She thought of herself awake, turning, her eyes raised to the sky, turning. She only wanted the turning to stop. She wanted to look straight ahead, to know where she was going. The turning, the eyes to the sky—it was impossible to find rest this way.

A gray smog hung over Konya the next morning when Yvonne boarded the bus. She was wrecked from a night without sleep. She had passed the dark hours tallying her mistakes, regretting things she had said and not said to her children, regretting coming to Turkey, regretting subjecting that beautiful boy to her broken, needy self. And now she was going to Ahmet's town with no notion of what she would do when she met his family. She had not rehearsed any words of explanation or condolence. Her mind raced through scenarios—the family shunning her, the family feeding her. The family condemning her, the family embracing her. Outside the bus window green haystacks were lined in neat, organized rows. She closed her eyelids, heavy with sleeplessness and sun.

Yvonne awoke to find her forehead pressed fast to the window. Outside was an impossible landscape. The bus had descended into a wide gray valley, flat but dotted with hundreds of spiked rock formations. Each was fifty feet high or more, and tapered upward, like a narrow volcano. She had never heard of such a place. She knew only that Cappadocia was mountainous. No one had told her it was filled with a field of hundreds, thousands, of stone chimneys extending as far as the eye could see.

The bus stopped. "Ürgüp, it is here," the driver called out. She disembarked, and the driver retrieved her suitcase and set it beside her. Dust rose up around her as the bus drove away.

A sign said CAVE HOTEL and pointed with an arrow, and she started the small climb up the hill. She would wash, settle in, and make a plan. It was still early in the day.

From outside, the Cave Hotel looked like a small mountain with a door. She rang the bell, and a minute later a man came out to greet her. He was in his early sixties, with neatly parted hair and a square chin. He introduced himself as Koray, the hotel owner, and told her they had one room available—a suite. "You are here by yourself?" he said.

He led her to a desk in a large room. It was only when Yvonne noticed the curved walls, the absence of windows, that she understood the room was a cave. She squinted at yellowish rings circling the gray chalky walls. Koray noticed her gaze.

"From volcanic eruption," he said. "This valley, these caves, made by volcanoes, and then the wind—" He gestured like a sculptor forming a torso from clay.

She filled out the paperwork he required. Koray led her down stone steps into a courtyard, and to another door. "This will be your room," he said. "One of the oldest caves in the region."

He unlocked the door and, once inside, switched on a light. He looked at the room with half-closed eyes, as though he didn't want to see any detail the housekeepers might have overlooked.

The room was cool and damp, with a small desk and a large, high bed. There were no windows. "Do you need anything else?" Koray asked, standing on the threshold.

"Actually, I wonder if you could help me," Yvonne said. "I'm looking for someone."

"Okay," Koray said.

"Well, I'm looking for anyone in the Yildirm family."

"I know Yildirms," he said, in a way that scared Yvonne. Had he heard of her role in Ahmet's death? "When you come upstairs, I have information for you."

She thanked him and closed the door.

In the bathroom, Yvonne held a small white hand towel under the sink faucet, and rubbed at her underarms, which smelled tart, and then between her legs. She removed her sandals and lifted one foot at a time to the sink before stepping on the bath mat. She gargled with the small bottle of mouth freshener supplied by the hotel, and spit. She avoided looking in the mirror.

She lay on the bed for a few minutes, staring at the cave around her. The bed was bordered by two night tables, each with lamps that had been turned on. She suspected she was the only person in the hotel who was traveling alone.

Upstairs, in the room where she had checked in, Koray was talking to an Italian couple about a hot-air balloon excursion. Yvonne spotted a computer in the corner of the room, its screen on, a stool set before it. She logged onto her e-mail, and was surprised to see a message from Aurelia. The subject header was, "Greetings from Istanbul." Istanbul! Her daughter was already here. Yvonne had no idea what day it was, or how Aurelia had arrived in Turkey so quickly.

She hesitated before opening the message. She tried to picture her daughter making the flight across the Atlantic, using her anti-anxiety pills, polishing the cuticles of her nails with oil (her cuticles cracked on airplanes, she claimed—a result of all the dry air). *Intimacy,* Yvonne thought, *was a ruse.* She knew a thousand pathetic details about her daughter, and still wouldn't be able to describe her accurately to a stranger.

She opened the message and immediately was relieved to find that in the first few sentences there was no trouble, no desperate need.

> *Mom,*
>
> *I made it to Istanbul and guess where I am? I'm staying at your friend Özlem's house! I called the number you gave me from the airport and she surprised me by telling me I could stay with her (extra nice since I looked into prices for hotels in this city and they're outrageous). Her place is really cool. Right by the Bosporous. She has such great things to say about you, but she also told me that maybe you're not in Datça?!!!*
>
> *She said that I should ask you where you are, and that if I don't hear back from you by this evening, she would tell me where you went. She said she wanted to give you a chance to explain things yourself, but that she didn't want me to travel to Datça tomorrow morning as*

I had planned if you weren't going to be there.

What is going on, Mom? This is so strange. We're supposed to join Matt on the boat in two days and I don't know what to do. I really think we should get you a cell phone that works internationally if you're going to keep disappearing like this. I know, I know. I'm one to talk. That's what Dad would say right now. But today I understand some of the fear that you guys must have experienced those times when you didn't know my whereabouts.

I guess what I'm saying is, please tell me what's going on and where I can find you! I'd like to hear it from you. All I can think is that maybe you've fallen in love with some Turkish man and have gone off to get married! Either that or you've been arrested, ha ha ha. Which is it?

xoA

Yvonne reread the e-mail. She could barely make sense of how Özlem and Aurelia had connected. All of it seemed impossible. But then, she had given Özlem's number to Aurelia. Why wouldn't Aurelia have called it? Yvonne was puzzled by her own surprise. Was it that Aurelia was suddenly so outgoing, so capable? Aurelia and Özlem were together in Istanbul, managing just fine, while Yvonne was in a moonscape of giant anthills, utterly lost.

When Koray was finished with the Italians he turned to Yvonne, and wrote something down and handed her the piece of paper. "Many of the Yildirm family have gone out of town," he said. "But one is here," he said, and pointed to the address. "Mustafa can take you."

"Okay, thank you," Yvonne said, taking the paper from him. She didn't know who Mustafa was.

"You wait here," Koray said.

Mustafa was a lanky man in his twenties, with gelled black hair. He leaned forward when he walked, as though pushing through a strong wind. "Madame," he said, and gestured toward the door.

Outside, she followed him to his car. He opened the passenger door for her and she got inside.

After he sat in the driver's seat she handed him the piece of paper Koray had given her.

"I know," he said, without taking the paper.

"Is it far?"

"No," he said. "You could walk but you would not find."

A tattoo with Ataturk's name circled his small bicep. He noticed her looking and pulled up his shirtsleeve. "His signature," Mustafa said, pointing to the etched version of the president's name.

"Very nice," Yvonne said, and quickly felt ridiculous.

The car was stuffy and reeked of cigarettes. She rolled down her window. They passed more of the strange formations—triangles with boulders on top. "What do you call those things?" she asked.

"Fairy chimneys," Mustafa said.

"What?"

"They look like chimney to home of fairies," he said. "The volcanoes come and then the wind shapes the lava like that. We get very strong winds that circle in the valley. The winds get stuck, like in a bowl. You see there is no green, no plants. Like a desert."

They passed a school, its courtyard empty now. *Ahmet must have gone there*, Yvonne thought.

"A school for girls," Mustafa said.

She couldn't decide whether she was disappointed. A part of her wanted to know every detail of what Ahmet's life had been like, and another part of her wanted to believe he hadn't left any mark on this town or its people.

The car pulled up to a large house built into the side of a hill. With an impressive balcony and heavy wooden doors, it was much grander than the other houses she'd seen. A small crowd was gathered outside the house, taking pictures. *It's made the news*, Yvonne thought. People were coming from all over Cappadocia to see where the boy lived. She imagined candlelight vigils at night, the tears of women glistening in the lights of the small flames.

"You like to get out," Mustafa said.

"Sure," Yvonne said.

If Mustafa hadn't said anything, she could have just as easily asked him to keep driving. The crowd of people surprised her. Would they know her face from the TV? She no longer resembled her passport photo—the picture, she assumed, that the journalists would have dug up to broadcast.

Mustafa said he would park across the street and wait for

her. He indicated a space next to a large bus—a tour bus. Yvonne had never imagined a scene like this. She assumed she'd be alone, or part of a small, intimate group, when she came to pay her condolences to Ahmet's family. She now saw there would be witnesses, judges of her behavior, just as there had been at the beach that day.

As Yvonne walked to the large front door of the house, she was intercepted by a woman of approximately Aurelia's age, her eyes heavily made up. The woman was talking to Yvonne while holding something in her hand—something black and narrow as a pencil. Another woman nearby shouted. She too was holding a small pencil-like object in her hand. Yvonne guarded her throat with one hand, her heart with the other. The first woman was very close to her face now, still speaking, and lifted her hands toward Yvonne's eyes. Yvonne felt something on her eyelids, something stinging, but did not fight back, did not push the woman's fingers away. *I deserve this*, she thought. *Whatever retribution or punishment this is for Ahmet's death, I deserve nothing less.* The woman's hands smelled of mint.

Yvonne could sense when the woman had stepped back—the sun was once more on her face—and she opened her eyes. She had not been blinded. The woman was smiling, nodding. She reached into her pocket and extracted a small mirror, which she held in front of Yvonne's face.

Black liquid makeup lined the tops of both eyelids.

"Like?" said the woman.

Yvonne didn't know what to say, so she nodded. The

woman smiled. Yvonne noticed that all the women outside the house had eyes that had been similarly lined. *A mourning ritual,* she decided. She felt sick.

She walked to the door of the house. No one stopped her. When she reached the threshold, she saw the door was ajar. She knocked lightly. A woman in her sixties, wearing heels, opened the door and said something in Turkish. She was wearing an expensive-looking silk blouse and a pearl choker.

"Mrs. Yildirm?" Yvonne said.

The woman looked confused.

"Oh," she said, after a minute. "Are you looking for Aylin?" Her English was excellent. Yvonne's relief was immense.

"I'm looking for anyone in the Yildirm family," she said.

"Aylin Yildirm works here, but not right now. Someone in her family has died."

Yvonne bowed her head.

"She's coming by today to get some things, though," the woman said. "She'll be here around five this evening."

"Thank you," Yvonne said, and stepped away from the house. "I'll come then."

She walked back to Mustafa's car. Who was Aylin? Ahmet's mother? What kind of work did she do for this woman? Mustafa was standing by the car, talking with another man and smoking. Both men had placed packs of Winstons on the hoods of their cars.

"It's not open?" said Mustafa. He was looking strangely at her face. Yvonne thought something was wrong until she recalled the eyeliner.

"What's not open?"

"The museum. You don't stay?"

"Museum?" Yvonne said, turning to look at the building again. There was no sign, save for a gold plaque near the front door. "What kind of museum?" she asked.

"The television program *Asmali Konak* was filmed here. In the house. Very famous. And now they make museum."

"A TV show was filmed here?"

"Everyone loves it. Is about the family with lots of money. People love seeing the rich so unhappy."

Maybe Ahmet's mother was an actress of some sort.

"Now there are other programs. Much more scandalous. Married women leaving their husbands. Every Thursday, women across Turkey watch to see the new possibilities for Turkish women."

Yvonne thought of Özlem.

"Can I take you somewhere else?" Mustafa said. "Another museum."

Yvonne was still piecing it together. The house was a museum to a now-defunct television show. And someone in Ahmet's family worked at the museum.

"No, not a museum," Yvonne said. "Is there somewhere else we can go? Can we see the fairy chimneys . . . or something?" Her voice sounded more pleading than she had expected. The truth was she didn't care where she went as long as it wasn't back to her room.

"In the afternoon is too hot to walk around fairy chimneys," Mustafa said. "You will see. It gets very, very heated."

She looked at his fingers on the steering wheel and noticed his hands were shaking. "Are you okay?" she said.

He looked at her and she gestured with her chin toward his hands.

"It's a problem I have," he said. "I once was a waiter and got fired the second day."

Yvonne nodded. Peter's hands had started shaking when he was in his forties. He tried to hide them, sitting on them like a child.

"I know a place that is interest to you," Mustafa said. "They are caves."

On the way to the caves, sand blew against the windshield. Mustafa turned on the wipers and leaned forward to the window so he could see. "We wait until the storm ends," he finally said, and stopped the car at a restaurant where the owners knew him. The restaurant had three floors, the bottom two filled only with empty tables. But the third floor was crowded with lunchtime diners, men in business suits and tourists in groups large and small. Yvonne and Mustafa sat at a table underneath a needlepoint of Ataturk's face.

"That is the picture you see the most because he smiles," Mustafa said. His own mouth frowned. "But more of the time he didn't smile, for a reason—he knew he had big job in front of him."

Mustafa continued on about Ataturk, how he walked and talked, how he was loved. Yvonne nodded often, happy not to speak. History was a comfort—it wasn't about her.

The food came and she ate and pretended to listen. Her thoughts were untethered, rising up in the heat. She was running through the sentences she would say to Ahmet's family, and none of them were adequate. She thought of the woman who had approached her door all those years ago, saying, "I want you to know that your daughter just landed my daughter in intensive care." Yvonne had not known how to respond, and not a month went by without her wishing she had said something, anything besides what she did say, which was, "Are you sure it was Aurelia?"

She thought of the woman who had killed Peter, how she too had been speechless. How she had said, "I have to go," before she disappeared.

When Yvonne started paying attention to Mustafa again, he was explaining why Ataturk never had children. "He did not want a dynasty. He did not want anyone trying to hurt him through his children. People might hurt his children, and he could not have this."

Mustafa paused, as though to see if Yvonne had been listening.

"Yes," she said absently. "People would do something to the children."

Yvonne paid the bill and they returned to the car. The wind had stopped and the heat of the day had peaked.

Mustafa drove a few more miles and parked in front of a row of tented shops, many of them selling carpets and embroidered blouses. He and Yvonne followed signs pointing toward the cave. The signs had been translated into many languages—Yvonne recognized the Italian word *grotta*.

"I have to tell you something," Mustafa said as they stood outside the entrance. "I cannot go inside with you. I am unable to be in there."

"Claustrophobia?" Yvonne said, and tried to explain what this was by placing her hands close to her head.

He nodded. She was relieved to be left on her own. "I will wait here for you," Mustafa said.

Yvonne turned toward an archway in a small mountain. "What am I seeing?"

Mustafa stepped toward her. "You will see underground city where Christians lived when they hid from the Arabs. Some lived entire life down there, never come up for anything."

Yvonne followed the tourists in front of her—a short man and his tall girlfriend. They seemed to be speaking German. She ducked as she walked down the steps of a tunneled passageway and found herself in a chamber of empty rooms. The ceilings were lower on each new level, and she continued to stoop. When she had descended four levels, the air was noticeably thinner. Yvonne had to inhale deeply. Some of the tourists near her turned back. "I don't need to see any more," she heard an American woman tell her husband. "I've gotten the idea."

Yvonne continued down through the tunnels, the ceilings becoming increasingly lower. She tucked her elbows in as the passageways narrowed. She passed through one room that had been a kitchen—she overheard a British guide saying so to his group—and she could see the soot on the ceiling above her head. She ducked through another chamber that must have been a church. She could still make out the crosses that had been etched onto the main wall. And it was here that she realized she was alone.

She needed to stop before moving on. She sat on the ground and pulled her knees to her chest. It was significantly colder now. She heard voices moving around her but couldn't judge their distance. The darkness was almost complete. What was she doing? She was seven or eight levels below the surface, lost in a soft-stone maze, alone. She was in Cappadocia, a place not included on any itinerary she'd made. She had traveled to Turkey to regain something of what she had had with Peter decades earlier—and failing that, she had befriended a boy. A Turkish boy who spoke nothing of her language. And now he was gone, and she was again searching for some remnant of someone she had lost. Had she ever been so lost herself? She must have seemed—to Özlem, to Ali, to Mustafa—profoundly so. A sad, aging woman with no anchor. Fumbling in underground caves.

Yvonne took in a deep breath, but it gave her no strength. She tried to inhale again, and felt nothing. She began to panic. Her voice called out and was echoed back at her. She didn't belong here. She needed to get back to the surface. Running as fast as she could, she ascended one of the narrow upward passages, and, while doing so, she hit her head. She touched her brow and felt her own blood. She kept her hand to her head and followed any upward ramp she could find. How far down had she been?

The light grew. She stumbled on, seeing more people as she made her way up the slippery stairs. Finally she emerged out of the mouth of the cave, gasping and coughing. She heaved so violently a stranger offered her his water bottle, and a woman put her arm on her stooped back. "You are okay?" the woman said.

"Yes," Yvonne said.

"Who are you with?" she asked.

"Um," Yvonne said. She was with no one. She looked up and saw Mustafa standing near the entrance to the cave.

"Him," she said, so relieved to see this man she did not know.

He reached his shaky hands to her and she walked toward them and held them until her hands and his were both still.

Mustafa found ice for her head and she held it close to her cut until the cubes began to melt. At five o'clock, Mustafa took her to the museum. She had not come to any conclusions about what she would say to Ahmet's relatives. It was only after she knocked on the museum door that she realized she didn't even have an opening sentence.

A young woman appeared at the threshold. "*Merhaba,*" she said, before saying something else. It sounded like a question.

"*Merhaba*. I'm looking for Madame Yildirm."

"Yes," the young woman said. "I am Madame Yildirm."

"Oh," Yvonne said. The woman was too young to be the boy's mother. "I think there's a mistake. I'm looking for the family of Ahmet Yildirm."

"Yes. I am his sister."

Yvonne was silent, staring at the woman's thin face. Her mouth was like Ahmet's.

"Can I help you?" the sister said.

"Sorry, my name is Yvonne."

"My name is Aylin. How can I help you?"

Yvonne took a breath. "I knew Ahmet. In Knidos."

Aylin's face seemed to narrow. Even the tips of her ears suddenly appeared pointed. "Come in," she said. "We can sit in here."

Yvonne followed her into a small room, a living room. The couch was a plush burgundy suede, and the room was filled with mirrors framed with elaborate, baroque metalwork. The photos on the walls featured what Yvonne assumed was the family from the TV show. The men wore fine suits and silk ties. The women wore black dresses, diamonds, and heavy liquid eyeliner. Yvonne now understood why the woman outside had painted her eyes—so Yvonne could look like she was on the television show. Aylin sat on the couch and Yvonne seated herself on a chair, its armrests painted gold.

"My parents are there now, near Knidos, getting his body," Aylin said. "They are bringing it back here for the funeral."

His body.

"How did you know him?" Aylin asked.

"Well, mostly I bought shells from him."

Aylin stood, and then sat back down. "So you're the one," Aylin said. "My grandmother told me about you."

"She didn't care for me."

"She doesn't care for anyone," Aylin said.

"I came to apologize," Yvonne said.

"For what?" Aylin's earrings, tiny diamonds, blinked.

"I feel it was my fault."

"Because you paid him to get shells?"

"Yes."

Aylin stared at her a moment and then laughed a short laugh. "You Americans." She flattened her skirt beneath her legs.

"What do you mean?"

"You think that everything has to do with you. That everything—good or bad—has its origins with you."

"But I paid him money for shells. I commissioned him."

"So you gave him money. He needs no money. He doesn't care about money. To him, it is a game. Let me tell you something about Ahmet. He always swims too far into the ocean, and jumps from high cliffs. He does what he wants to do. This is why he was sent to be with my grandmother. He has always been this type that causes my parents trouble. You, you are just someone who wants to think you have an effect on someone's life. On a young Turkish boy's life."

The conversation was not following the path of any of the scenarios for which Yvonne had prepared herself. She was acutely aware of the touch of the couch beneath her. Her mind was stunned, her body still.

"Why did you come here?" Aylin said.

"Because—because I know what it's like," Yvonne said. "I lost my husband two years ago. And I liked your son—I mean, your brother. I know what you must be going through."

"You don't know what I'm going through. How can you know? Everyone's grief is different."

Yvonne closed her eyes against the coming tears. "I'm sorry." She stood to leave.

"Sorry," Aylin said. "I didn't mean to be so—"

"There's no reason for you to apologize," Yvonne said. "Really. I expected anger. In fact, I think I came here to receive your wrath. It would almost make me feel better."

"I can't do that for you," Aylin said. "But I will tell my family that you were here. They will be glad to know."

Yvonne was out of words. She smiled, the tears overtaking her. She stepped out the door and ran to Mustafa's taxi and was gone.

Back at the hotel, Yvonne was greeted by Koray.

"I have a question," she said. "How far is it to Datça?"

"To get anywhere by plane, you fly to Istanbul first. There are many flights each day. A little more than an hour by plane to Istanbul, and then to Datça, I don't know. An hour and thirty minutes maybe. Are you going there?"

"Not now," Yvonne said. "I'll go tomorrow."

Koray looked out at the sky and Yvonne followed his gaze. Three clouds formed a row of dots—an ellipsis.

Before she returned to her room for the night, she logged onto the hotel's computer and wrote to Aurelia.

Aurelia,
That's wonderful that you found Özlem. I will meet you and your brother on the boat, as we agreed. I'm not in Datça now, but I will be there in time. I promise.
Love, Mom

She was tempted to write more, but how could she explain her friendship with Ahmet, and his death, in an e-mail? She would see Aurelia on the boat and tell her everything then.

Her cave room was cold. In the mirror she saw the paint on her eyes was smeared. She was washing her face when the phone rang.

"Oh good. It's you." It was a female voice. "All roads lead to Mustafa."

"Excuse me?" Yvonne said.

"Everyone knows Mustafa. He told me where to find you." She paused. "It's Aylin, Ahmet's sister."

"Yes," Yvonne said. She sat down on the bed.

"I want to apologize for the way I talked to you today. It was kind of you to come."

"Thank you," Yvonne said, and suddenly lost her breath. She wanted to fall into the arms of Aylin. "Please, do you think . . . can we talk some more? I don't know what I want to say, but I want to tell you about him, about your brother, if you like. I liked him very much. He was a beautiful young man. I could tell you stories of his time in Knidos . . ." Yvonne felt ridiculous. "I only say this because after my husband passed away, I wanted to know everything about him, any detail anyone knew."

There was a long pause.

"I would like that," Aylin said. "You could come to the museum or I could come to the hotel tomorrow."

Yvonne tried to picture them talking on the patio of the hotel, next to guests making inquiries about camel rides, or in the museum where Aylin worked, under the disapproving gazes of a wealthy and troubled family. Yvonne felt trapped by rooms, by caves, by Westerners wanting to live like Turkish people and Turkish people wanting to live like Westerners. "Can we go for a walk tomorrow?"

"We can walk in the valley beneath the castle," Aylin suggested. "I go there often. It's not far from your hotel."

"Okay," Yvonne said. "What time?"

"Eight in the morning?" Aylin suggested.

"I'll see you then," Yvonne said.

"Yes."

"Thank you for calling," Yvonne said, but Aylin had already hung up.

Yvonne awoke early the next morning, hungry from not having eaten the night before. She dressed in turquoise, her missionary dress. She left the coolness of the cave room and walked into the accumulating heat of the day. The sun, an ancient coin, was rising over the horizon.

An elderly couple sat at a table near Yvonne's. They both had white hair cut the same short length. The woman was plump and the man was thin, his legs long and pale.

"I'm thinking when we get home," the woman said, "we should plant some orange flowers by the front hedge." She had a faint Southern accent.

"Why orange?" said her husband. He was eating eggs. She was eating yogurt.

"I saw it in a magazine," said the woman. "I saw some orange flowers and they looked really . . . uninvasive."

"I know you're worried about invasiveness."

"I just think orange would be nice. Or maybe red."

"I think it's really going to make a difference," said the man. "A big difference."

"You don't have to be so negative," said the woman.

"That fountain worked out great," said the husband.

"I said it before and I'll say it again. I like it. I think it's nice."

"It sounds like someone's perpetually pissing in our garden."

The woman appeared as though she might speak, but

then thought better of it. Instead, they both turned sullen, like punished children.

Yvonne knew their anger, recognized it instantly. She and Peter had spoken to each other like this toward the end of his life. It had been easier to justify their resentment of one another when Aurelia was causing them strife, but when she turned twenty-one and turned sober for good, and they still didn't get along, they had no one to blame but each other. And so they fought. They fought about how much money to leave as a tip at an Ethiopian restaurant. They fought about whether or not a student should have been expelled for cheating on his SATs. They fought about the placement of the rug in their living room, about Yvonne's tendency to leave half-full glasses all over the house. They had grown so accustomed to resenting each other that they didn't know how to stop. And they could no longer blame Aurelia.

The white-haired couple had finished with breakfast. Their chairs screeched against the patio, and Yvonne avoided looking at them as they returned to their room. She stared at the cave houses before her, in the near and far distance. They were all crumbling, and Yvonne couldn't decide if the view resembled a civilization at its start or its finish.

◇ ◇ ◇

Mustafa drove Yvonne to the valley. The landscape was lunar, everything white and gray, the rock formations seeming more illogical and make-believe now with their shadows so long.

"Should I wait here?" Mustafa asked.

Yvonne declined. She knew the way home.

She stared at the many entranceways that had been carved into the mountains. She could make out Turkish flags hanging above many of the doors. People still lived there.

"Hello," a voice behind her said. It was Aylin, dressed in a silk blouse and a black skirt. Aurelia would have approved of the silk.

"Are you okay to take a walk? I don't want your clothes to get dirty."

"There's a café in one of the chimneys," Aylin said. "We can go there."

They walked down the narrow path of sand.

"I feel I should apologize for just showing up at your work yesterday," Yvonne said. "I shouldn't have shocked you like that."

"I was not prepared," Aylin said. "But I didn't need to be so rude. I don't blame you for what happened to my brother. But I wanted to ask you how you recovered from death."

"From Ahmet's death?"

"No," Aylin said. "You said yesterday that your husband died. I am curious what you did to make it easier. My family, you see, they are all devoted Muslims. They have the mosque, and my father will cleanse my brother's body there before the burial. And Ahmet will be dressed as though for his circumcision. He will wear a suit and a hat, and have a baton. And across his body there will be a sash that says *Masallah*.

It means, 'May God Protect.' But I am not religious. I don't believe what they believe—I decided that long ago. But their faith is giving them structure now. Answers. A way to go through this. I feel different. I have no answers."

Aylin was sweating in the heat, and small wet circles appeared down the back of her blouse, where her spine touched the silk.

"Should we sit?" Yvonne said. Even this early in the morning, the sun was punishing.

"Yes, good idea," Aylin said. "The café is in there." She pointed to the fairy chimney to their left and they walked inside the main archway. Immediately it was cooler. Yvonne followed Aylin up a staircase, carved into the stone, and they emerged into a shallow room lined with books. At the end of the room was a balcony, where they sat on a cushioned bench.

A young boy approached them, and he and Aylin exchanged a few words. "Coffee?" Aylin said to Yvonne, who nodded. Aylin said something else to the boy, and he walked away.

"I don't know how to answer your question," Yvonne said. "I had a lot of help when my husband died." As soon as she said it, it sounded false. She had not had a lot of help. She had only had Aurelia. "It was my daughter," Yvonne said, working out the thought as she spoke. "It was her. She brought order to things. She was . . . miraculous."

And suddenly it was clear. It had been Aurelia. In the aftermath of Peter's death, Yvonne and Matthew had braced themselves for Aurelia's reaction: most of her life, she would have used even a parking ticket as an excuse to drink, to steal, and accuse, and throw tantrums. When Peter died, Yvonne and Matthew had made sure Aurelia was not alone. With a real excuse, she seemed capable of anything.

And yet it was Aurelia who had been calm. Who could have known that in the face of real tragedy Aurelia would thrive? It was as though now that everyone else was finally living in the realm of passion and intensity with which she had conducted her life, she was at peace. Matthew and Yvonne turned to Aurelia for solace. It was Aurelia who washed the dishes and made the beds and stocked the kitchen with tea and milk and starches (that was all they could stomach then: bread and rice, the diet of sick children). It was Aurelia who had dealt with the life insurance company, with the questions from the police, the details of the funeral. It was Aurelia who had opened the windows to let in fresh air, and calmly told off the telemarketers who called and asked for Peter.

Yvonne finished telling Aylin all this, and the young woman nodded reverently, as if she had been told the story of a magnificent hero of history. "She is strong, your daughter," she said.

"No," Yvonne said. "Actually, I guess yes. She never used to be. But something changed." It was only now that Yvonne understood this to be true. Her daughter had changed a long time ago—even before Peter's death. It was only Yvonne's idea of her that had remained unaltered. She had not opened her eyes to her daughter in years. Aurelia was no longer a broken thing to be tinkered with. She was a woman, a person, and Yvonne needed her.

The boy brought them their coffee in small teacups. Yvonne looked toward the other fairy chimneys, at other tourists sitting on other balconies, being served by the very people who had once called these bizarre structures their homes.

"You just need to wait for the days to go by," Yvonne said. "It might be hundreds of days, a thousand, but one day, you find that the pain has dulled. That it no longer clouds everything you see."

"It was like that for you?" Aylin said.

"Yes," Yvonne said. She was lying. That day had not come yet but she hoped that it was not far off.

When they finished their coffee, Aylin had to go. Yvonne said she would stay in the café a little longer. Aylin reached for her purse to pay, but Yvonne stopped her.

"You know the path back?" Aylin asked.

"I'm fine," Yvonne said. "I know the way."

They parted with kisses on each cheek. Aylin smelled like Yvonne's daughter: a simple scent, like dried flowers. Yvonne inhaled it, filling her lungs before they parted. From the balcony, she watched as Aylin appeared on the path below and made her way to the road, to her small car parked at the trailhead, near a stand where a young girl was selling fruit.

Yvonne paid the boy for the coffee and went out to the path once again. She hadn't decided whether to walk back to the hotel yet. She wound her way between the stone towers, touching them, looking for people in their hidden windows. She wondered idly if they had always lived here, if the mothers and sons and fathers and daughters watched from within as their homes were scoured by the swirling gusts of wind. She touched the walls, felt the scars of the years, the centuries.

As she wandered, the breeze picked up, making a whistling sound as it wove around the rocks. The air grew coarse with sand. She lost the path in front of her. It happened quickly. Yvonne's vision blurred. She rubbed her eyes. She was in the middle of a sandstorm and could not see more than a few feet in front of her. She tried to walk back in the direction of the café, but saw nothing of the way she'd come. The squall spun itself into frenzies.

She ran to the base of a fairy chimney and sunk to the ground. She would wait out the storm. She breathed into the cavity created between her lap and her knees. Whenever she lifted her head, she saw only dust. What in god's name had happened to her? She could not be trusted to walk alone in a landscape like this. It occurred to her that even if she were to stand and run, she would not know which way to go. She sat for an hour or more, the storm unrelenting. Would she die here? She could be swallowed in this place, she realized. She could be lost here because she thought she knew the way back—that she, always the teacher, always the mother, could never need the help of another. This had been her way for too long. She could not listen. It had been so long since she listened, since she allowed those close to her to show her anything new. Everything had been written long ago. Her children! She had treated them as facts, as figures in an unchangeable story—a lesson she knew and could teach.

Finally, the whistling stopped. The wind died. When she raised her head, the dust caked her face, covering her tears. She needed to find someone who would help guide her to shelter. But who would she find? Who would help her, and how? She was alone here, and would remain alone. She opened her eyes. Sand stuck to her lips. In the distance she saw a figure walking toward her. She was unsure, at first, whether it was someone coming to help or someone who also had been caught in the storm. She stood and tried to breathe. Was it a man or a woman? A boy or a girl? The figure came closer. It was a woman. Her shape was familiar. Yvonne recognized her walk. It was a woman who had come to rescue her. She knew this woman. She had made this woman.

"Mom," Aurelia said, her arms outstretched. "Oh, Mom."

Acknowledgments

Books make their way to publication through the vast generosity of dozens of people, from editors to production staff to friends who agree to read the manuscript in its earliest and most awkward stages.

I had many friends willing to gaze upon, and suggest improvements to, this novel in its early and inelegant forms: Ann Cummins, Nancy Johnson, Andrew Leland, Lisa Michaels, Cornelia Nixon, Ron Nyren, Ann Packer, Ed Park, Angela Pneuman, Michelle Quint, Sarah Stone, Ayelet Waldman, Amanda Eyre Ward, and Sally Willcox. Thanks also to Jenny Moore and Soumeya Bendimerad.

While I was in Turkey, I had wonderful companions, Linda Saetre and Heidi Julavits, who traveled with me on boats and buses and in cars, and put up with my many detours.

Thanks also to Rabih Alameddine, Alev Lytle Croutier,

Sevim Karabiyik, and the friends I made in Turkey, all of whom answered questions technical and cultural.

I'm grateful to my agent, Mary Evans; and to all at Ecco: Dan Halpern, Virginia Smith, Allison Saltzman, and everyone else at this serious and vigorous house. Thank you also to my UK editor, Karen Duffy.

My family was patient and supportive during the years of research and writing that this novel required. Thank you especially to my husband, Dave; my sister, Vanessa; and my parents, Paul and Inger Vida.